THE SPIRIT OF CATTAIL COUNTY

VICTORIA PIONTEK

THE SPIRIT OF CATTAIL COUNTY

VICTORIA PIONTEK

SCHOLASTIC INC.

ISBN 978-1-338-34647-3

12 11 10 9 8 7 6 5 4 3 2 1   18 19 20 21 22 23

Printed in the U.S.A.   40

Originally published in hardcover by Scholastic Press, June 2018

This edition first printing, September 2018

Book design by Nina Goffi

FOR MY MOM, ELIZABETH,
WHO LOST HER OWN MOTHER
WAY TOO SOON

CHAPTER ONE

They buried Sparrow Dalton's mama the day the fortune-teller came. A day so hot, some say the swamp started to bubble. The water of the Everglades rose in the air and hung there, a steaming mist that cloaked the little town of Beulah in a persistent haze.

Sparrow watched as they lowered Mama's casket through the lingering precipitation and into the ground. As the casket creaked and swayed on the ropes that held it fast, vapors swirled in a way that had nothing to do with the weather. Among those rising vapors, Sparrow searched for Mama. She felt with deep certainty she would see Mama again, and she had good reason for this conviction.

Sparrow saw spirits.

In fact, she had seen one ghost, the Boy, with such life-long regularity and clarity that he was as sure as the beat of her young heart.

He was with her even at that moment, as real and as solid as the preacher who presided over Mama's grave. His features were so unlike the murky wisps of typical spirits that she marveled no one else saw him. Though the two of them had always been different. She, a girl who looked at death. He, a ghost who looked like life.

For Sparrow, the only reminder that he was a ghost was his impenetrable silence. He was her greatest secret, yet he told no secrets himself.

She wished he would tell secrets. For if he could talk to her, then it would have been a simple matter to ask after Mama. Sparrow wanted to know where Mama had gone. More important, she wanted to know when Mama would return. Because if the Boy could live side by side with Sparrow, spending long summer days trailing her about the house like a dog, then so could Mama. She knew it wouldn't be exactly as it was before. Sparrow wasn't crazy enough to think that. She only wanted to see Mama again so she wouldn't miss her so much.

Sparrow was so lonely for Mama that her soul ached like a thumping drum, and without Mama, Sparrow had no one to love her.

Sparrow had no sisters, no brothers, and no daddy. Truth be told, she had no true friends either. Sparrow had the misfortune of being an anomaly in a town that took offense at difference. Beulah had never forgiven Sparrow for being born on the same night as the great flood. It seemed folks found it hard to separate her arrival with the rise of the swamp waters. It felt like a bad omen.

To make matters worse, she had the nerve to show up bearing no resemblance to her fair mama. Sparrow had eyes the color of cattails and black hair that twisted like reed grass. Beulah folks joked that Sparrow must be the daughter of the swamp itself to be washed ashore in the flood and so different-looking from Daltons born in generations past. Of course, they wouldn't have speculated so, if Sparrow had a Beulah-born daddy or Mama had stopped the rumors as fast as they'd started. Mama had a defiant streak, though. She'd refused to talk about Sparrow's daddy, and the story stuck.

With Mama gone, Sparrow's only claim to friendship and family were the ghost of a silent boy and Auntie Geraldine, her only living relative.

Sparrow liked the idea of having an aunt. She just didn't like the one she got.

Auntie Geraldine was a force to be reckoned with. A force she applied liberally and often to Sparrow, as she was doing now. Auntie Geraldine pinched the back of Sparrow's arm, for the preacher waited for Sparrow to come forward and cast the first handful of dirt on Mama's grave.

Sparrow had made it clear before they left the house that morning that she wouldn't do this. It was one thing to bury Mama, quite another to throw dirt on her.

Auntie Geraldine smiled up at the preacher and then gave Sparrow another pinch.

Sparrow clamped her hands on the sides of her chair and looked resolutely at the horizon.

A few awkward seconds passed, during which the preacher mopped the sweat from his brow with a hanky and Auntie Geraldine looked around with a forced smile.

Finally, the preacher said, in an overly indulgent and patient way, "Perhaps, sister, you can take her place."

Auntie Geraldine gave an assuring nod and rose, her thin, bony body as strong as steel. She straightened her starched skirt. Paused. Then looked at Sparrow.

She reached out, cupped Sparrow's chin in her hand, and pressed her nails into the tender skin of Sparrow's cheeks before turning to do the preacher's bidding. Auntie Geraldine was good at many things, but was at her best when keeping up appearances.

Auntie Geraldine grabbed a handful of freshly turned soil and held it in her palm. The Boy moved so close to Auntie Geraldine that they were almost touching, and bent down. He put his mouth right next to her palm, as if he would kiss it, and blew. The soil lifted on a ghostly breeze, swirled playfully in the air, and fell like raindrops to the ground.

Auntie Geraldine glared at Sparrow.

It was almost as if she suspected it was Sparrow's fault.

Sparrow glared back, unjustly accused.

She no more controlled the Boy than she did the weather, although she was grateful to him. She hadn't wanted to throw dirt on top of Mama, and now she realized she hadn't wanted anyone else to do it either. Somehow, the Boy knew it. So maybe, in a way, she did control him.

Most likely not. Spirits are fickle things.

CHAPTER TWO

Midday faded into twilight and Beulah said goodbye to Mama, though no one but Mama remained at the little road-side cemetery anymore. The funeral party had progressed from graveside to Sparrow's family home.

Sparrow lived in a ramshackle, two-story house the Daltons had owned for more generations than she could count. It sat at the edge of the wetlands, and despite the family's attempts at upkeep, its white paint had a perpetual gray tint that flaked at the edges. Every spring they slapped a fresh coat of white paint on the house, but by midsummer, the salt from the nearby brackish water wore it right off. That's how life was near the wetlands, a continuous cycle of corrosion and renewal.

Sparrow never minded about the color. She liked the way the gray boards peeked out from under the white. It looked better to her like that. It looked lived in and well loved, and Sparrow sure did love her house. She loved everything about it. She loved the way the tin roof clanged during thunderstorms, the thumping rain so loud it sounded like angels tap-dancing overhead. She loved the way the porch encircled the house, wrapping it tight with a screen like a protective cocoon to keep out the mosquitoes and the gnats that infested the marsh. She even liked the way the screen door slammed shut, lumber slapping loudly against lumber, but she reserved her deepest affection for the creaky porch swing. Crafted from cypress wood so old it was practically petrified, it hung from the rafters by braided rope as thick as a man's fist.

Sparrow sat on her petrified porch swing in black mourning clothes bought for the funeral. The swing swayed gently, propelled into motion by the Boy's ghostly magic. More a familiar than a ghost, he lounged beside her on the swing, and together, they watched the mourners, two souls set apart from the rest.

All of Beulah, it seemed, turned out for Mama's funeral. On this day, the Monroes, the Castos, and the Daltons commingled in a way that wouldn't happen under other circumstances. Death brought Beulah's founding families together in a way that births and marriages did not.

If there had been fewer people crammed into the confines of Dalton House, and less chatter, Sparrow would have heard the telltale clicking of Auntie Geraldine's heels as she searched for her errant niece. Sparrow was supposed to be accepting condolences and nodding politely. Instead, she was hiding in plain sight to avoid talking to folks about Mama because it made a lump rise in her throat and tears sting her eyes despite her belief that she would see Mama again.

If she'd heard the sound of those heels, she would have gone somewhere else, but as it happened, she did not, and Auntie Geraldine caught her like a fish on a line.

"Sparrow Dalton!" Auntie Geraldine said.

Sparrow stiffened. The sound of Auntie Geraldine's voice dragged down her spine like nails on a chalkboard.

Auntie Geraldine approached Sparrow and peered down at her from her lofty height. Auntie Geraldine was a tall woman. She rose to an impressive height of five feet ten inches without heels. In them, she reached six feet or more, depending on the shoe. In Sparrow's opinion, Auntie Geraldine was too tall to wear heels, but she wore them all the time anyway.

"We discussed this," Auntie Geraldine said. "You can't mope around. It makes people uncomfortable." Manners and appearances were of utmost importance to Auntie Geraldine.

"I don't feel like talking," Sparrow answered, matching her aunt's terse tone. Though small-boned and delicately made, Sparrow resembled her namesake in more than just build. Like the hearty brown birds that flitted in and about the house eaves, Sparrow's grit surpassed her size, a trait that annoyed Auntie Geraldine to no end.

"Stop that infernal swinging," Auntie Geraldine said.

Sparrow used her foot to stop the swing's ghostly sway.

The Boy cast her a petulant look.

She ignored him.

Auntie Geraldine sighed impatiently. "As hosts, we have a responsibility to our guests. To their comfort while in our home."

The use of the word *our* in reference to Sparrow's home irked her. Auntie Geraldine had moved back into Dalton House the last weeks of Mama's sickness and had been lording over it ever since. Dalton House belonged to them, Sparrow and Mama, not Auntie Geraldine. It was like the worst kind of take-backsies, and in her meaner moments, Auntie Geraldine threatened to sell Dalton House to the highest bidder.

Mama's leaving had turned Sparrow's whole world upside down in more ways than one, and the only way it'd ever be set right again was with her return.

"I'll go to my room," Sparrow said.

"Absolutely not. People will think you are hiding."

Sparrow *was* trying to hide, but she didn't say this to Auntie Geraldine. Instead, she struggled to hold the swing still and to keep her efforts from showing in her expression.

The force of the swing pulled at her ankles like the out-going tide. The Boy liked to tease Auntie Geraldine, making things move when they should stay still, and his antics made Auntie Geraldine mad at Sparrow.

"Appearances matter, Sparrow. Your mama's passing has brought up the old gossip, and I'll not have the Daltons being the talk of the town. It's hard enough living in this house again without having to listen to that ridiculous story." Unlike Sparrow, Beulah loved to ponder the identity of her father. Sparrow felt it smacked of disloyalty to Mama to think on it too hard. She wouldn't mind knowing, she supposed, but if Mama didn't care to discuss it, then Sparrow didn't either.

"I've already spoken to every—" Sparrow lost control of the swing. It swung backward and rocketed forward toward Auntie Geraldine. It hurled into her, nearly knocking her off her feet.

Auntie Geraldine caught the rope and jerked the swing to a stop. She was a formidable woman, carved from stone, and the hit wasn't enough to topple her. Auntie Geraldine looked around to see if anyone noticed. Several people dropped their eyes when her exacting gaze veered their way. In Beulah, someone was always watching.

"Why must you make everything so difficult?" Auntie Geraldine hissed. "If you refuse to do what's expected of you, then go into the yard with the kids. At least that way, you won't be moping on this swing, making people feel sorry for you."

"Fine." Frustration tainted Sparrow's response. She didn't want to go into the yard with the kids or wander the house talking to the adults. She wanted to sit quietly on her swing and let her thoughts drift toward Mama. She expected Mama to appear at any moment now and wanted to be waiting when she did.

Auntie Geraldine cleared her throat and raised her eyebrows expectantly.

"Yes, ma'am," Sparrow corrected herself. Auntie Geraldine reminded Sparrow of a rattler. She warned before striking, and Sparrow knew when to withdraw. The prudent walked around a coiled snake rather than step over it.

"Good," Auntie Geraldine said, going to the screen door. She held it open and seared Sparrow with her glare.

The Boy dissolved like mist in the midday sun.

Coward, Sparrow thought as she watched him go. He never stuck around to witness the fallout of his pranks.

Auntie Geraldine tapped her foot impatiently.

Sparrow rose from her swing. *From the frying pan into the fire*, she thought begrudgingly as she walked into the yard where the Beulah kids waited.

CHAPTER THREE

Sparrow leaned against one of the giant oak trees that shaded her yard. The leafy canopy of the ancient trees grew thick near the house and dripped with Spanish moss. Over the centuries, their wandering roots had snaked toward the marsh, gradually claiming the land for their own and creating Dalton dirt. Dalton dirt was a salt-and-pepper mixture of soil and sand, suitable for only the hardiest of trees and random tufts of crabgrass.

On this flecked terrain, the kids of Beulah played a game of baseball beneath the oaks' protective shade, but Sparrow had no intention of joining them. She knew without asking that she wasn't invited.

Instead, she looked past them to the marsh. Flat and wide, it stretched deep into the horizon and buzzed with life. Birds and insects, gators and snakes, reed grasses and fishes all thrived in their marsh. The Daltons owned it all, as far as the eye could see, but Florida swampland held no monetary value. Sparrow kept its only worth locked up in her heart, and with it, the hope that Auntie Geraldine's threats to sell the house would wilt like hydrangea in the mid-day heat. Sparrow couldn't even consider the idea of living anyplace other than Dalton House—her home, the Boy's home, Mama's home.

The sound of a bat hitting a ball drew Sparrow's attention away from the marsh to the kids. The game they played had been going on for a while, long enough that most of them had likely forgotten the reason they were at her house in the first place.

As night moseyed toward Beulah, the sun slunk slowly down the sky, but enough light lingered for them to play ball and the choking heat didn't matter. These kids were Beulah raised. The effects of fevered temperatures and strangling humidity hardly bothered them.

She lifted her mass of black hair off her neck, releasing the heat trapped beneath as she watched Johnny Casto step up to home plate.

Johnny took his place under the oak tree that served as home base in their makeshift game. He hoisted an old board over his shoulder and nodded to his sister, Maeve, who waited on third. They both had the Casto red hair, and it flamed in the glow of the setting sun.

Andrew Monroe claimed the pitcher position and read-ied his throw. He drew his arm back and raised his knee.

He took a focusing breath and his face turned grave with a seriousness unwarranted for a friendly game of ball, but then, the divides separating the folks of Beulah chafed like chiggers.

Like their parents, the kids were split into two groups. The first group was the Castos, a sprawling, half-wild clan of redheaded siblings and cousins that no one could ever keep straight. The second was everyone else.

Unlike most of Beulah, Sparrow liked the Castos. She didn't care that they went almost everywhere barefoot and had a reputation for fighting. She understood how it felt to be outside of a circle she should have been in.

As a Dalton, Sparrow's place in the world should have been secured, but Beulah liked sameness. Sparrow reeked of difference. For starters, she had picked an unlucky night to be born. Then she'd had the nerve to look different than expected. Two transgressions that likely would have been forgiven in time if it hadn't been for the Boy.

She walked with him, and he left his mark on her. Even when the Boy left her, his presence lingered like a scent. Sparrow carried the faintest whiff of death, a peculiarity that made people uncomfortable even if they blamed other factors for the cause. For this reason, Beulah kept its distance from Sparrow, and Sparrow had grown accustomed to life on the sidelines.

Maeve Casto shouted, "Bring me home, brother," and scooted off third in an attempt to steal home.

Andrew swung around and threw the ball to his twin sister, Ansley, who manned third base. Ansley leaped in the air, easily snatching the ball. Both the twins were athletic and had the honey-blond hair and blue eyes that Beulah prized. They were the perfect examples of Beulah pedigree— polite, golden, and old-money wealthy. Too bad they were also snarky, sneaky, and gossipy.

Maeve dashed back to third before Ansley could tag her out.

Ansley huffed and tossed the ball back to her brother.

Maeve smirked devilishly and wiped the black eyeliner that always rimmed her eyes even on the hottest days. Maeve had five older sisters and was privy to secrets most girls Sparrow's age didn't know.

Sparrow considered clapping to show her support for the Castos but then thought better of it. Even though she felt a kinship with them, they felt no allegiance to her. Only Castos belonged to Castos. Just because they weren't enemies didn't mean they were friends.

"Quit messing around, Maeve," Johnny hollered, and choked up on his bat.

"Just bring me home, brother." Maeve rubbed her hands together like she could already taste victory.

"No cheating, Castaway," Andrew called.

"What'd you say?" Maeve asked, leaving third base and making a beeline for Andrew.

"Maeve, get back on base. It's what they want." Johnny dropped his bat and started after his sister.

"I said, no cheating, *Casta-way*," Andrew answered, emphasizing the long-running insult. Beulah regularly called the Castos the Castaways behind their backs, but few dared to say it to their faces. Doing so was asking for a whipping. Both the girls and the boys had quick tempers and even quicker fists, and Maeve was the meanest of the bunch.

Maeve took one step closer to Andrew and met him eye to eye, her freckled nose just above his. Maeve was going to be a sixth grader in the fall, the same as Sparrow, Johnny, and the twins, but only because she'd been held back a year. This meant that even though Andrew was tall for his age, Maeve topped him by four fingers. She also fought better.

Maeve poked Andrew in the chest. "No one calls me a cheater or a Castaway."

"I call it like I see it," Andrew said, and then tagged Maeve with the ball. "OUT!"

Ansley whooped.

Maeve looked ready to spit fire.

Sparrow felt riled up herself.

16

Mama's death, Auntie Geraldine's ill nature, the threat to Dalton House, the heat—all sparked and crackled like kindling, feeding an anger she'd been unaware of moments before. She was tired of things she couldn't control. She wanted to exert her will on something and a cheating Monroe fell smack-dab into that category.

She started toward Maeve and Andrew just as Johnny trotted up beside his sister. Johnny tried to pull Maeve away. "Forget it. We're still ahead."

If Maeve was the meanest of the Castos, Johnny was the kindest. Sparrow had never seen him start a fight. In fact, he'd often try to broker peace if it could be found, but if it couldn't, his fists were as hard and as swift as any Casto's.

Andrew grinned. He seemed to think the odds had swung in his favor now that Johnny was there to control Maeve. "Yeah, Maeve. Be a good girl and listen to your brother," he said, his good ol' boy drawl as plain as his good ol' boy smirk.

Sparrow reached the pitcher's mound just as Maeve shoved Andrew.

In seconds, the entire outfield rushed toward them to watch the impending fight. They formed a tight circle around Andrew and Maeve. On either side of Sparrow, shoulders pressed close. In their excitement, the kids beside her forgot to keep their usual distance, and for that single moment, she belonged.

Then a sulfurous breeze traveled across the marsh and touched Sparrow's hair. A tendril tickled her face. She moved to brush it aside, reminding the kids on either side of her of her presence. The kids pushed away, forcing the circle into a crescent. Sparrow, alone, remained in the yawning space like a raft adrift on an unfriendly sea.

She ignored the rejection. The idea of Andrew Monroe thinking he was better than other folks made her blood boil. "Andrew Monroe, apologize to Maeve right now!"

"Andrew? Maeve started it, *swamp rat*," Ansley said, tossing her glove on the ground and planting herself in front of Sparrow like she wanted a fight too.

"You know that's not true," Sparrow said.

"Swamp rat and Castaways sitting in a tree. K-I-S-S-I-N-G," Ansley singsonged.

"Shut your mouth, Ansley," Johnny said. "For goodness' sake, her mama just died."

Sparrow didn't know what shocked her more: a Casto sticking up for someone outside of their family or the embarrassed flush that turned Ansley's cheeks red. Sparrow had never known Ansley to regret an insult.

Maeve looked from Ansley to Andrew, balling and unballing her fist as if she couldn't figure out which Monroe she disliked most. Suddenly, she seemed to decide and flew at Andrew, pouncing on him like a wild animal.

They toppled to the ground, brawling like tomcats.

Andrew yelped in pain. "She bit me!"

"Oh, boy." Johnny reached down to grab his sister by the arm.

Sparrow pushed past Ansley and reached for Maeve's other arm. She'd about gotten hold of it when the spectating kids scattered.

"The grown-ups are coming," Johnny said.

Sparrow glanced toward the house and instantly regretted taking her eyes off the fighting pair, because in that second of inattention, Maeve and Andrew rolled toward her and knocked her off her feet.

She tried to scramble out of the way, but before she could, Andrew's elbow slammed into her mouth, making her teeth rattle, and her head hit the ground.

To Sparrow's relief, a hand grabbed her by the forearm and dragged her out of the fight. Gratitude washed over Sparrow as her limbs disentangled from Andrew's and Maeve's, but when she turned to face her savior, her relief turned to dread. She hadn't been rescued. She'd been caught by Auntie Geraldine.

Auntie Geraldine's alabaster cheeks burned a furious red, and her eyes bulged in disbelief. "Sparrow Dalton!

I believe you have just about lost your mind!" That she yelled in front of company gave testimony to the depth of her anger.

Sparrow's lip throbbed, and she tasted the metallic tang of blood. Andrew's elbow had cut her lip. She opened her mouth to say something, but one look from Auntie Geraldine silenced her.

Mason Casto hauled Maeve off Andrew. Mason Casto was Maeve and Johnny's uncle, and he looked as angry as Auntie Geraldine.

Wesley Monroe reached out an elegant hand to help his son up. "You all right?" he asked kindly. As the town's only lawyer, he owned the biggest, prettiest house in Cattail County. He did all the law in Beulah, of course, but also worked in Havisham, which was why, according to Auntie Geraldine, they had so much money. A tidbit Sparrow knew to be fact since Auntie Geraldine kept track of things like that.

"Fine," Andrew said through gritted teeth.

He didn't look fine. Dirt covered his white dress shirt, and both eyes were swelling. He did his best to brush himself off and then turned to Auntie Geraldine. "Sorry for the trouble, Ms. Dalton."

"I know it wasn't *your* fault." Auntie Geraldine smiled at Andrew in a kindly way that made her look like Mama.

When she smiled like that, her ice-blue eyes warmed, and her hair seemed more blond than gray, but it was a smile Sparrow rarely saw since Auntie Geraldine never bestowed it on her.

"What happened here?" Wesley Monroe asked.

"Nothing," Sparrow, Johnny, Andrew, and Maeve said in unison. None of them would talk to the adults about what happened. Every kid in Beulah lived by one rule—tell the grown-ups nothing. Kid business was kid business, and as such, they dealt with things in their way. There'd be paybacks, but they would happen far from the adults' watchful eyes.

"Welp, if no one is talkin', I'll take these two home," Mason Casto said. "You can rest assured, Geraldine, we'll handle this at our place."

"I would hope so." Auntie Geraldine turned her stony gaze toward Sparrow. "As for you, young lady, we'll discuss this in private."

"Go easy on her. No real harm's been done and she just buried her mother," Mason Casto said.

"I most certainly will not. Acting in such a despicable way on today of all days. It's inexcusable! My sister is probably rolling over in her grave."

The reminder of Mama in her grave felt like a punch in the stomach, and Sparrow's knees buckled. Auntie Geraldine

21

didn't need to say such awful things. She only did it to hurt Sparrow.

Mason Casto reached over and steadied Sparrow to keep her from falling. "Geraldine," he said softly.

"I'll not be lectured at by a Casto," Auntie Geraldine snapped, and everyone felt the yoke of Beulah's social structure. Castos didn't tell Daltons how to act, even when the Dalton was in the wrong.

Mason nodded, and after an uncomfortable pause, he offered his hand to Wesley. "Sorry about your boy there."

Wesley returned the gesture, and the two men shook. "He's tough. Aren't you, son?" He slapped Andrew on the back.

Andrew nodded miserably. Maeve had clearly beaten him.

The Castos turned to leave, and everyone watched as they walked away. They got in their truck, and Mason Casto maneuvered it out of the long line of cars parked in the Dalton drive.

He started to pull out onto Route 17. Then he stopped to make way for a vintage van, the color of periwinkles, hauling a teardrop camper. It zoomed down the rural country road toward town.

"Flea market folk," Wesley Monroe said.

"*Charlatans*," Auntie Geraldine corrected him.

As Sparrow watched the blue van speed by, a girl leaned out the window and released a piece of yellow paper, as if setting a bird free. The paper took flight. It fluttered back and forth, making the most of its freedom. Just when it looked as though the paper would land in the middle of the road, the swamp sent a breeze its way and the paper picked up momentum again, hurtling toward the funeral party like tumbleweed. As it flew by, Sparrow snatched it from the sky.

It was an advertisement. THE GREAT MADAME ELENA was typed in bold at the top of the page, and below the words were three tarot cards. Under the cards, more text said, *Be amazed. Be astounded. Child psychic. Sees all. Knows all. Have your fortune foretold and all your questions answered. Appearing for a short time only at the flea market.* Then much lower down and in much smaller print: *All readings $20.00. Cash only, paid in advance.*

A quiver of curiosity quickened in Sparrow's stomach—*sees all, knows all.*

Auntie Geraldine ripped the paper from Sparrow's hand. She scanned the page and then tore it down the middle. *"Fortune-tellers,"* she said, her disdain clear.

Fate, Sparrow thought.

CHAPTER FOUR

On the third day after Mama's funeral, Sparrow awoke to a bright blue sky streaked with cotton clouds stretched so thin they were almost mist. The sun hummed with heat and Sparrow felt betrayed by nature's reminder that life marched on.

The night of the funeral had been awful. Auntie Geraldine claimed Sparrow behaved so abysmally that she must not have any Dalton blood running through her veins whatsoever. A hateful comment that stayed with Sparrow in the days that followed, burrowing like a beetle since she feared the truth of it. Sparrow had always known she was half Dalton and half something else, but she always thought of herself as a Dalton. Now, without Mama to tether her to the only family she'd ever known, the connection felt fragile. Especially when Auntie Geraldine questioned her suitability to the family name, and the mirror cast its own doubts.

Sparrow sometimes wondered if Mama *had* conjured her out of the swamp, creating a creature entirely of her own invention. An invention with parts so unlike any Dalton ever crafted, Sparrow struggled to see how she fit. Where Mama was fair, Sparrow was dark. When Mama's blue eyes sparkled, Sparrow's brown eyes cast shadows that threatened black. While Sparrow's dark curls twisted in tangled brambles, Mama's blond hair rested in quiet repose. Sparrow didn't want to change the way she looked. She simply wanted her looks to *profess* her Daltonness.

She needed Mama now more than ever.

Mama had yet to show herself to Sparrow, and the waiting tore at her in a way that frayed her edges. She missed Mama so hard her insides hurt and her bones ached. She wanted Mama back, and the Boy's presence proved Mama's death didn't have to be the final goodbye.

Before Mama passed away, the Boy had simply been part of Sparrow's world like the oak trees, the porch swing, and the wetlands. Like these things, he had existed as just another thread in the tapestry of her life at Dalton House, but now his manifestation hinted at more—a bridge to the other side, a key to a locked door, a promise of what could be.

Sparrow wanted the Boy's reborn existence for Mama, but she didn't know how to make it happen. She wished the Boy would seek Mama out and show her how to become like him. She wondered if there was a way to get him to teach Mama his tricks.

She sighed, unsure. The Boy had always refused to be controlled.

Sparrow thought about the yellow flyer drifting her way the night of Mama's funeral. To Sparrow's knowledge, a fortune-teller had never come to Beulah before. Her arrival, at the very moment Sparrow needed help, was a bit of luck too good to be coincidence. A fortune-teller must know a thing or two about spirits. She might even know how to make the Boy help Mama, or better yet, how to lure Mama back. To find out what the Great Madame Elena knew, Sparrow simply needed to visit the flea market in Beulah.

And today she was going into town with Auntie Geraldine.

Sparrow generally preferred to walk to town, but Auntie Geraldine liked to drive. She owned a gold Buick. A large, gas-guzzling car so pristinely clean and icebox cold that riding in it felt a lot like being trapped in the frozen food aisle at the big supermarket over in Havisham. Traveling in the Buick rated among the more unpleasant experiences in Sparrow's new life with her aunt, but the cold interior wasn't the only reason Sparrow disliked the car rides. They also took forever.

Sparrow could have walked to town faster than Auntie Geraldine drove there. Auntie Geraldine took her time on a drive, savoring every inch of the short distance between points. When it only took ten minutes to get everywhere they needed to go, there was never a reason to rush. This meant that Sparrow sat uncomfortably close to Auntie Geraldine for an uncomfortably long period of time.

Auntie Geraldine put the key in the ignition and the car in drive. The automatic locks clicked assuredly, and they were slowly on their way.

Sparrow spun around to look out the rear window. The Boy leaned against a massive oak, staring out at the marsh as if soaking up the view. Apparently, he disliked Auntie Geraldine's car rides as much as she did since he had chosen to stay behind. The Boy did what he wanted, and in that moment, Sparrow envied his freedom.

Auntie Geraldine swatted Sparrow. "Sit right."

Sparrow sighed irritably. Auntie Geraldine's touch stung like nettles. She rubbed the spot, trying to soothe her skin, and then slid around, turning her back on the Boy.

When they got to Main Street, Auntie Geraldine pulled up in front of Long's Drugs and stopped.

Auntie Geraldine reached into her purse and handed Sparrow four dollars. "You go on in there and buy yourself some lunch while I meet with Wesley Monroe. I'll pick you up when I'm done."

Sparrow couldn't buy lunch at Long's with four dollars.

"Is he going to read Mama's will?"

Auntie Geraldine snapped her purse shut. "What do you know about wills?"

"I watch TV and read books. Mama might have said Dalton House was mine."

Auntie Geraldine tapped her fingers on the steering wheel impatiently. "We've been over this. She didn't leave a will. You're going to live in Havisham with me, and if Dalton House can be sold, it's going on the market."

Sparrow toyed with the four dollars, folding and unfolding the bills. "Mama loves Dalton House."

"And I *loved* my sister, but she never thought ahead. Lord knows why a woman dying of cancer wouldn't prepare a will, but that sums up your mama. Now I'm left trying to fix what should have never been left unfixed to begin with." Sparrow knew Mama had loved Auntie Geraldine, but she never thought about Auntie Geraldine loving Mama back. She doubted Auntie Geraldine had it in her to love anyone.

Sparrow stared out the window at Long's. Surely, Mama had a better plan. Leaving her in the care of grouchy Auntie Geraldine seemed haphazard at best, and Mama never would have considered selling the house.

Sparrow reached for the door handle and paused. "Maybe I should hear what he has to say anyway."

Auntie Geraldine pinched the bridge of her nose. "For

heaven's sake, Sparrow. Do as you're told for once. You make everything too hard."

Sparrow got out of the car and stuffed the four dollars into the pocket of her shorts. In Sparrow's opinion, Auntie Geraldine was the one who made things too hard.

Auntie Geraldine rolled down the passenger-side window and leaned across the seat. "Wait for me here." She looked at her watch. "It's eleven now. I should be about an hour. And no wandering. That shady flea market is in town and I don't like those people."

Sparrow dug her hands deep into the pockets of her shorts. Mama never had a problem with the flea market or the flea market people. In fact, Mama and Sparrow went together every year.

"All right," Sparrow said.

Auntie Geraldine cleared her throat. "Yes . . . ?" she prompted.

"Yes, ma'am," Sparrow answered.

Auntie Geraldine rolled up the window and drove off.

Sparrow watched the car glide leisurely down Main Street like a boat drifting in a current. When the Buick faded out of sight, Sparrow turned and hightailed it down Main Street.

She had an entirely different destination in mind—the flea market.

The flea market came to town every July and set up in the empty field near the 76 station. Vendors drove in from all over. Like nesting birds, they erected makeshift booths next to their vehicles, and for that one month, tourists from the far reaches of Cattail County and beyond flocked to Beulah.

Beulah folks loved the flea market too. Everyone enjoyed poking through the bric-a-brac with the hope of finding a priceless treasure. Every July, Mama and Sparrow would spend Sunday afternoons wandering through the stalls looking at the wares for sale. Sparrow always got the sense that Mama searched for something in particular that eluded her year after year, but whenever Sparrow asked, Mama declined to confess disappointment. Instead, she'd say, *I have everything I could ever want* and pull Sparrow close, kissing the top of her head.

Sparrow didn't have time to poke around for treasure this trip, though. She needed to find that fortune-teller and return to Long's before Auntie Geraldine. Like an army colonel, Auntie Geraldine demanded obedience. Disobeying a direct command was unwise.

As Sparrow searched for the periwinkle van with the teardrop camper, she wove through the array of stalls that had little rhyme or reason to the goods hawked. Old bicycle parts were on display next to outdated clothing. Mismatched silver was offered next to vinyl records. One booth even sold faux fur coats in vivid colors. Just looking at them made Sparrow hot.

Sparrow finally spotted the vintage van and the camper on the far side of the field. She hurried in its direction.

On one side of the van, a booth had been set up with a sign that read RARE ANTIQUITIES, and though filled to the brim with all kinds of items for sale, it was unmanned. On the other side of the van, a silk party tent had been erected. Two of the sides were tied back to make a door. Above the makeshift door, a sign written in a kid's hand dangled precariously. It read THE GREAT MADAME ELENA.

A girl about Sparrow's age sat at a table under the purple silk.

The young fortune-teller wore a floor-length sundress, layers upon layers of jewelry, and glamorous movie star sunglasses. Her chestnut-colored hair hung in long, loose waves that made Sparrow wish she had run a brush through her tangles.

Simply spotting the fortune-teller made Sparrow's excitement surge. She had been to the flea market every year of her life and never had there been a psychic before. Her arrival, when Sparrow needed help, felt like fate. More than that, it felt like divine intervention by Mama. As if Mama sent the fortune-teller to help Sparrow find the way across the divide that separated them.

Miss Ruby Long, the owner of Long's Drugs, sat across from Madame Elena and listened intently as she spoke.

Sparrow did her best to wait her turn at a polite distance, but found herself inching closer and closer to get a better view of the young Madame Elena at work.

Madame Elena spoke to Miss Ruby with a lively energy, using her hands to help convey her meaning. With each movement, her bracelets jangled and her rings sparkled. She pointed at a tarot card and said, "You've had a long, interesting life."

Miss Ruby laughed. "Truer words have never been spoken."

Madame Elena smiled at Miss Ruby and then darted a look at Sparrow.

Sparrow hadn't realized how close she'd gotten to the purple tent. She now stood only a few paces away. She quickly turned her head and started whistling a nameless tune as if she had no interest whatsoever in the conversation taking place under the tent. She whistled several bars of her made-up song and then casually swiveled back around.

Both Madame Elena and Miss Ruby watched Sparrow.

Sparrow's whistle petered out like a broken horn. She hadn't fooled anyone with her pretend nonchalance.

Miss Ruby winked at Sparrow.

Madame Elena gave her an exasperated look and got up. "Readings are private." She released the ties holding open the door, and the purple cloth rippled closed, cutting off Sparrow's view.

Sparrow tried to wait patiently, but the longer it took, the more anxious she became about making it back to Long's before Auntie Geraldine. Sparrow had gone AWOL and Auntie Geraldine did not have a forgiving nature. Sparrow's mind swirled with the punishments Auntie Geraldine might devise for her—polishing silverware during a lightning storm, endless meals of stone-cold grits, raking up moss filled with chiggers, and unknown consequences that Sparrow knew were possible but couldn't foresee.

This last category made Sparrow's stomach twist.

She paced anxiously while Madame Elena and Miss Ruby talked in the privacy of the purple tent.

Finally, Miss Ruby emerged.

"Good morning," Sparrow said, as Miss Ruby walked her way. Sparrow adored Miss Ruby. Like a lot of Beulah kids, Sparrow often found herself sitting at Ruby's lunch counter riveted to the spot by her stories. Miss Ruby wove a masterful tale. Her ancestors had survived slavery and she'd marched on Washington to fight segregation, so she had a lot to share. Miss Ruby once told Sparrow her experiences shaped her view on things, and Sparrow knew this to be true. Miss Ruby treated kids like they had the same rights as grown-ups, and spoke to them as if they could make up their own minds about things. Even Beulah's youngest citizens valued that kind of treatment.

"Sorry about eavesdropping," Sparrow said. Miss Ruby was always direct, which made Sparrow want to act like her.

"Never mind about that. It's good to see you. You've been on my mind. You holding up okay?" Miss Ruby patted Sparrow on the shoulder. Sparrow appreciated that Miss Ruby didn't draw away from her like most folks. If Miss Ruby felt uncomfortable around Sparrow, she never let it show.

Sparrow nodded. "I guess. You didn't come out to the house after the funeral."

"No," Miss Ruby answered, and then paused. "Your folks and my folks. You know how it is."

Sparrow did. By folks, Miss Ruby meant black and white. It wasn't that Beulah didn't mix. They lived side by side in a small town. It was that they didn't mix in every way. Sparrow knew Miss Ruby went to her own church and her own social events. Life in Beulah was like the rings of a tree. There were so many circles within circles, it made Sparrow's head spin. "I missed having you there."

"I'll miss your mama. She was a sweet soul."

"Thanks." Sparrow wanted to say something more to show how much Miss Ruby's words meant to her, but she had to bite her lip to keep from crying, so she couldn't speak for a moment.

Miss Ruby seemed to understand and moved the conversation toward something easier to talk about. "Are you here to have your fortune told? You're in for a treat if you are. That girl has a gift."

As if on cue, Madame Elena tied back the doors to her tent and began to tidy her space. She rearranged the unlit candles on her table and snapped a red cloth theatrically before letting it float down over her tarot cards. "Don't forget to tell ALL your friends," she called to Miss Ruby.

An amused smile pulled at Miss Ruby's lips. "You'll only get rave reviews from me, dear."

Madame Elena beamed with pleasure at Miss Ruby's compliment, and then sat down at her little table. She clasped her hands in front of her as if she expected Miss Ruby's friends to arrive immediately.

"*That* good?" Sparrow whispered, her expectations soaring.

Miss Ruby leaned in conspiratorially. "One of the best, I suspect. Comes from a long line of fortune-tellers."

Sparrow nodded knowingly, even more impressed.

"Don't forget to tell me how it turns out." Miss Ruby patted Sparrow on the shoulder again and left.

Sparrow slid into the empty chair across from Madame Elena. "I'm here for a consultation."

Madame Elena took off her movie star sunglasses and arched a nut-brown eyebrow. "Hmm . . . That's interesting because it seemed like you were here to spy on me."

Sparrow cringed. She felt scolded, which was odd since she was sure Madame Elena was the same age as her. "No. That was accidental. Sorry."

Madame Elena leaned forward and looked into Sparrow's eyes, holding her gaze as if searching for signs of deceit. Sparrow wondered if Madame Elena could read minds. After several uncomfortable seconds, Madame Elena sat back and grandly announced, "Forgiven."

"Thank you," Sparrow stammered before she realized she had thanked another kid for forgiving her for spying. Every kid Sparrow knew spied. It was the only way they learned anything.

"You're welcome." Madame Elena smiled like a pardoning angel.

Sparrow felt a tick of ire at Madame Elena's benevolence and refused to utter the second "thank-you" that threatened to escape from her lips. Instead, she asked, "Does everyone call you Madame Elena?"

"Just Elena. The Madame part is homage to my grandmother. She was the original Madame Elena. But it also looks good on the flyer, don't you think?" She pulled a yellow flyer off a stack next to her and slid it across the table.

The bold black letters spelling out THE GREAT MADAME ELENA did look good against the yellow flyer, but Sparrow didn't think Elena was actually asking her opinion.

"What do people call you?" Elena asked.

"Sparrow."

Elena lit a candle. "Well, Sparrow. I can see that you have many questions that need answers." She spoke quickly and assuredly, a stark contrast to the soft, slow way Beulah folks talked.

"I do," Sparrow agreed, impressed Elena could tell she had a lot of questions just by looking at her.

Elena nodded sagely and her dangly earrings swung. "You've come to the right place. Twenty dollars, please."

Sparrow hesitated. She had forgotten all about the money. She reached into her pocket and pulled out the bills Auntie Geraldine had given her. "I only brought four dollars with me. Anything I can get for that?"

Elena looked at the crumpled bills skeptically. "That's not much."

Sparrow crossed her fingers and willed Elena to agree to something. Sparrow's need to see Mama grew more intense by the hour. In the days since Mama's funeral, some details had already slipped away. Sparrow could no longer recall the exact tone of Mama's voice or the precise way Mama's hand felt in hers. Each second that ticked by made Sparrow feel like she was losing Mama bit by bit, like sand slipping through an hourglass.

Elena considered her. Sparrow wondered if she looked as desperate as she felt. Elena sighed. "I sometimes do one-card readings."

Sparrow didn't hesitate. "I'll take it."

Elena tossed her enviable hair over her shoulder with a sophistication that made Sparrow feel the tug of her small-town roots. "You don't even know what it is. How do you know you want it?"

"Okay, what's a one-card reading?" Sparrow asked without much care. She felt grateful to be getting something. She didn't have the money to haggle and she knew whatever the fortune-teller said would be important.

"You think of a question while you pick a tarot card. The card you pick will be the answer to your question."

"Deal." It was perfect.

Elena held out her hand.

Sparrow put the crumpled-up dollars in Elena's palm and her faith in the tarot cards.

CHAPTER FIVE

Elena deftly shuffled her cards. Her hands moved swiftly and skillfully as she manipulated the deck. The cards were lovely. Cream colored with black filigree that twisted and coiled along the edges, they had the nimble pliability of well-worn paper. These cards had been loved with an affection Sparrow recognized. She felt the same way about her cypress porch swing.

"I like your cards," Sparrow said.

Elena paused her shuffling to look at the deck. "Thanks. My grandmother gave them to me. They were hers when she was a girl."

"Miss Ruby mentioned you come from a long line of fortune-tellers."

"I do," Elena said proudly. "My grandmother learned from her grandmother, and her grandmother learned from her grandmother, and . . . well, you get the idea." Elena held her cards in one hand and used the other to accentuate her story. "It goes on and on for generations." With each movement her bracelets clanged together.

Sparrow liked the way Elena's bracelets jangled when she moved. Sparrow had never worn jewelry. She didn't even own any. "Is your mother a fortune-teller too?"

Elena scoffed. "Not even close. She's a professor back home in New York City. In my family, fortune-telling skips a generation. My grandmother didn't even try to teach my mom. She said she could tell the moment she looked into her forthright, guileless eyes that she didn't have the spirit of a mystic."

Sparrow wondered if she had inherited her ability to see spirits from family. If she had, she didn't have a clue who it came from. It wasn't Mama. "Does your mom wish she was a mystic like you?"

Elena smiled dolefully. "No. She thinks it's ridiculous."

"Does she mind that you tell fortunes?"

Elena pondered the question. "She wishes I was more interested in science, but my mom is a feminist. She says girls face enough obstacles as it is without people telling them what they can and can't do." As Elena talked, she shuffled her cards with an absentminded precision that indicated hours of practice. "Besides, as my grandmother always told her, card reading is a gift from the women in our family . . . a skill they picked up to survive when women had few options for making money and being independent."

Despite her quick cadence, Elena spoke about her heritage in a very Beulah-like way.

"Did your mom bring you to Beulah?"

"No. My uncle. The antiquities booth over there is his." Elena motioned toward the booth on the other side of the periwinkle van. She finished shuffling her tarot cards and set them on the table. Then she leaned toward Sparrow and inhaled. "Are you wearing perfume?"

"No." Sparrow brought her hand to her nose. She didn't smell anything.

"I'm catching a whiff of something that smells like roses, only not quite. It's not bad or anything, just a little sad. Can a smell be sad?" Elena shrugged. "Anyway, are you ready?"

Sparrow nodded.

"Think of the question you want answered," Elena directed.

"Is there a trick to picking the right question? You know, like in stories when a character is granted three wishes by a genie? They always ask for the wrong things."

"I know! Why do they do that?" Elena's face brightened and for a moment, she seemed like a normal kid. More like Sparrow's age than someone older and wiser. Then Elena's demeanor shifted. She became earnest and commanding as she slipped back into her fortune-teller role. "This is kind of like that. The better the question, the better the answer. Try to be specific."

There were so many questions Sparrow wanted answered, but all of them boiled down to the same basic one—how to make Mama become like the Boy.

"Got it?" Elena asked.

"I think so."

Elena knocked on the deck of cards three times and then spread them on the table in a long row. She waved her hand over the cards like a magician. "Spirits near, spirits far, spirits old, spirits new, come now and guide the seeker's hand." She focused on Sparrow. "Now let your intuition guide you as you pick a card."

Sparrow waited for a moment to see if any spirits arrived. This seemed like just the thing the Boy would love, and Elena had given a direct invitation. When Sparrow felt positive that no spirits had answered the call, she studied the cards, trying to decide which one to pick.

Sparrow took her time. She didn't want to make a bad choice. Then one card appeared to flutter a little bit. The wiggle was so slight, Sparrow didn't even know if she actually saw it move or imagined it. No, she decided. The card had moved.

"That one."

Elena removed the card from the row and scooped up the rest of the deck, setting it aside. She flipped the chosen card over and put it between them.

"You drew the Page."

Sparrow examined the threadbare card. The faded picture depicted a young boy in medieval clothing.

"In the olden days, a page worked for a knight. They did many jobs, but one of the page's most important tasks was carrying messages. Often when a page shows up in a reading, it means you'll soon be receiving a message or that someone is trying to tell you something," Elena explained with an air of authority.

A feather of excitement tickled Sparrow's stomach.

"Do these words have meaning for you?" Elena asked.

Sparrow pulled the card closer to her and examined the picture. It wasn't an exact answer to her question. It didn't tell Sparrow how to make Mama like the Boy, but it was the promise of a connection. The page was a messenger, and that meant Mama *was* trying to contact her. *Would* contact her. Sparrow's heart picked up speed. "They *do!*"

Elena smiled triumphantly. "Tell your friends that Madame Elena knows all."

"You got it," Sparrow promised, forgetting she didn't have any friends to tell.

Elena pushed back her chair.

"Wait! Can you tell me what the message is?"

"Not without a more in-depth reading, and that costs twenty dollars. I'm not running a free advice booth." Elena stood.

Sparrow got the hint. She had gotten her four dollars' worth. If she wanted more information, she needed more money. Not the easiest thing to come by, but Sparrow would figure out a way to get it. She had to. "I'll be back."

"I'll be here." Elena moved to the tent door and folded her hands in front of her, waiting for Sparrow to leave. She looked like a church usher.

Sparrow wanted to say something that would encourage Elena to tell her more, but despite Elena's friendly smile, it was clear Sparrow was being dismissed.

Reluctantly, Sparrow said her goodbyes and started walking toward Long's.

She practically floated through the flea market, admiring the items for sale as she went. For the first time in days, she felt truly hopeful and less lonely. The Page card made it clear that Mama was trying to make contact. Now she just needed to figure out what Mama wanted to tell her.

Sparrow stopped at a jewelry booth manned by a portly vendor with a sunburned nose. She picked up a gold-plated pocket watch and looked at the face. Both hands pointed at the number twelve. Sparrow showed the watch to the vendor. "Does this have the correct time?"

"It does. Even a broken watch is right twice a day." He chuckled at his own bad joke and pointed at the watch Sparrow held. "That one is correct at midnight and noon."

Sparrow looked up at the sky. The sun was directly overhead. "It's noon *already*?" The vendor looked at the watch he wore on his wrist. It was a modern digital version that apparently functioned perfectly all day long. "On the nose." Her thoughts from earlier came rushing back and Sparrow's mind whirled with all the punishments Auntie Geraldine might inflict on her. Like before, it was the unknown consequences that scared Sparrow the most and made her stomach twist. Sparrow shoved the broken pocket watch at the vendor and took off running.

She was late.

CHAPTER SIX

Sparrow sprinted the entire way to Long's even though the noonday sun throbbed with heat and the humidity hung in the air so thick it had weight. At times, Beulah's humidity took on an oppressive nature, hovering over the little town with a relentless stickiness that clung to everything.

Sparrow skidded to a stop in front of the drugstore. As she scanned the cars parked along Main Street, her heart pounded against her chest, struggling to adjust to the sudden change in pace. When she saw no sign of Auntie Geraldine's Buick, she felt an instant wave of relief. She'd made it.

She took a few deep breaths to slow her racing heart and pushed open the door to Long's. The bell at the top of the door rang softly, and the AC blasted her with an arctic breeze that felt divine against her hot, sticky skin.

Sparrow let the AC cool her for a couple of minutes and then started to make her way to the back of the store.

Long's was more than just a drugstore. It sold a lot of different things folks in Beulah might need in a pinch, like milk, eggs, and batteries. It also sold things kids liked. It had a rack of books and comics, bins of candy sold by weight, and cheap toys that broke after a day. From eleven to two, Monday through Saturday, they served lunch. Long's was such a multipurpose location, Sparrow hadn't even known Long's Drugs actually sold medicine until Mama got sick. After that, she couldn't think of it as anything other than a drugstore.

Long's divided its services into four tidy sections. It devoted the front of the store to the lunch counter. This ran along one side of the building near a row of four booths with red, cushiony seats. Across from the booths, a series of well-ordered shelves held groceries, and behind the dry goods, the kids' area spanned a horizontal row that ran parallel to the pharmacy counter.

Even though it was always busy at lunchtime, the place was unusually packed. Tourist and flea market folks filled the booths and sat at the lunch counter.

Miss Ruby maneuvered past Sparrow with a tray of burgers, and then paused to look at Sparrow. "You walk through the swamp to get here?"

Sparrow pushed her sweaty hair off her face. "Ran all the way from the flea market. It's hotter than the sun out there."

"Ah, the energy and folly of the young," Miss Ruby mused. "How'd it go with the fortune-teller?"

"Amazing, like you said." Knowing that Mama was trying to contact her made Sparrow feel twinkly, like she was dancing with fireflies.

Miss Ruby shifted the tray of burgers. "Tell me all about it when I'm not so busy."

"You got it." Sparrow ducked under Miss Ruby's tray and went to the kids' section, where she could wait out of the way of the hustle and bustle of the lunch rush.

She stopped at the book carousel and slowly spun it around, looking at the novels for sale as if she could afford one.

Sparrow didn't know where she would get twenty dollars for a more in-depth reading. Money had always been a problem for Mama and Sparrow. Mama never made Sparrow feel deprived for basics, but there rarely seemed to be quite enough to make ends meet. The Daltons had standing in the community because they were a founding family, but they hadn't had money in generations.

Auntie Geraldine might dress ritzy, drive a nice car, and own her own house in Havisham, but Sparrow knew those were leftovers from better days. Auntie Geraldine used to be married to a businessman, but he died. Auntie Geraldine cherished all of her belongings from her time with her husband and took great care to keep them pristine, especially her Buick.

48

Sparrow had gone through one complete spin of the book carousel when Maeve and Johnny burst through the front door of Long's and dashed toward the kids' section.

Maeve and Johnny ran past her and slid behind the candy bins like they were stealing home plate. They ducked out of sight. Then Maeve popped out again, grabbed Sparrow by the arm, and yanked her behind the bins.

"Get down." Maeve pulled Sparrow into a crouch.

Sparrow tore her arm from Maeve's grip. "What in the world are you doing?"

"Ansley and Andrew," Maeve hissed.

Sparrow peeked over the candy bins. "So? They're not even out there."

Maeve jerked her down again. "But they're *coming*."

While Sparrow preferred to avoid the twins because of their unpleasant natures, she didn't usually hide from them. "Who cares if they see me?"

Maeve rolled her eyes. "You would if you had any sense."

"Those two have been tracking us all over town ever since . . ." Johnny trailed off.

Maeve took up the story. "You know, the baseball game the other day . . . at your house. They put word out that they're going to pay us back good. Normally we wouldn't be running, but . . ." Maeve shook her head. "Lordy, our uncle was mad. Said if we stirred up any more trouble we'd be

49

scrubbing out grease spots at the 76 station for the rest of the summer."

Maeve and Johnny's uncle Mason worked at the one-pump gas station near the flea market.

"He said *you'd* be scrubbing out grease spots for the rest of the summer. I don't recall him saying anything about me," Johnny countered. "I wasn't the one fighting like a tomcat, remember?"

Maeve glared at her brother. "Us running has made them brave."

Just then, the bell over the top of the door chimed. Maeve, Johnny, and Sparrow peered over the candy bins.

Maeve pointed at the twins, who were standing near the lunch counter. "If you're so confident Uncle Mason was only talkin' to me, go over there and take care of things so we can enjoy the rest of the summer."

Johnny ignored his sister and scanned the store. "Back door." Johnny pointed past the pharmacy counter toward the hall that led to the bathrooms.

Sparrow knew Long's had a back door, but it never occurred to her she'd have reason to use it.

"Come on." Maeve crouched low, and crab-walked to the hallway.

Johnny followed and then turned to Sparrow. "Are you coming?"

Sparrow was taken aback. She kept up with the endless skirmishes and battles that defined life for Beulah kids, but she'd never been a participant before. "Do you think they're out to get me too?"

"You picked sides and it wasn't theirs," Johnny said. "You want to wait here to find out?"

"No. I don't," Sparrow said, and followed Johnny. She hadn't consciously picked sides the night of Mama's funeral. She had defended the Castos because the Monroes cheated and it was the right thing to do, but she liked being lumped in with them even if it meant she was on the run from the Monroes.

Once Maeve, Johnny, and Sparrow escaped out the back door, none of them seemed to know what to do next. The three kids stood around, awkwardly looking at each other.

"I guess I'll see you two later." Sparrow gave them a wave and turned to leave. She wasn't sure how far this newly formed alliance went, but she didn't think it included joining the Castos as they roamed Beulah on a summer afternoon. Besides, Auntie Geraldine would be back for her soon.

She was walking away when the back door flew open.

"RUN!" Maeve shouted, and took off with Ansley hot on her heels.

Johnny and Andrew looked at each other for a half

second before Johnny said, "Darn it," and charged toward Sparrow. As he raced past, he grabbed Sparrow's shirtsleeve and pulled her in the opposite direction of Maeve's retreat. "COME ON!"

Sparrow saw Maeve disappear around the far corner of Long's with Ansley right behind her. Divide and conquer seemed to be the Castos' strategy for keeping free of the twins' clutches. Sparrow agreed wholeheartedly with their tactic and put all her effort into running.

Though small, Sparrow ran fast, and once she started sprinting, few kids in their grade could catch her. To her total surprise, Johnny matched her step by step. She hadn't known he could run fast. She'd never seen a Casto run before. They usually stood their ground.

When she couldn't hear Andrew's footsteps on their heels anymore, Sparrow looked behind her.

Andrew had stopped quite a ways back. He stood hunched over with his hands on his knees, huffing and puffing. While Andrew excelled at football and baseball, sports that required brute strength, his size worked against him in a footrace.

Sparrow and Johnny kept running until Andrew's hulking form shrank to gnat size and then they slowed to a jog.

Their mad dash had taken them all the way down Main

Street and onto the old country road that ran out toward Sparrow's house.

Suddenly, Johnny stopped cold.

"Are you worried about Maeve?" Sparrow wondered if Johnny regretted separating from his sister. Divide and conquer had its advantages, but also its drawbacks. Johnny and Sparrow had escaped Andrew, but now Maeve might be running around Beulah with two fuming Monroes in pursuit instead of one.

"Nah, that girl's tougher and has more lives than a feral cat. It's just . . ."

Johnny trailed off and Sparrow realized where they were—the little roadside cemetery . . . where Mama was buried.

CHAPTER SEVEN

Sparrow walked across the field of green grass dotted with tiny headstones, and Johnny trailed silently behind her. A hot breeze blew. The trees overhead quivered, making sunlight dapple across her face, and she felt the touch of spirits. Their presence alighted on her skin, like dew on grass.

Only a few locations in Beulah attracted spirits—the quiet, shady lane next to the 76 station, the dark corner of the marsh at the bend just before town, and the tiny graveyard. These places drew them like moths to a flame. The entities that collected in these spots were fragile, fleeting creatures that had little in common with the Boy.

The Boy seemed to be a different species altogether. Unlike those fragile, smoky wisps, he thrived. Unbound to place, he did not shudder and sway with the wind but endured in a form so solid he practically lived. If he could only speak to Sparrow, he'd cross the one divide that separated them.

The Boy gave Sparrow a glimpse of what could be, and she latched on to the prospect like a life preserver. Being in the cemetery flooded Sparrow with grief. Memories of Mama's casket being lowered into the ground hit Sparrow like a set of waves, pummeling her over and over again with an unrelenting force that threatened to pull her under. When Mama found a way to be like the Boy, Sparrow wouldn't have to hurt so much anymore. Most days, Sparrow's chest felt so tight with the ache in her heart she could barely breathe.

Sparrow wove through the headstones until she reached Mama's spot. It wasn't hard to find. Diminutive and weather worn, the cemetery's size reflected the town it served. Mama's freshly dug grave, with its mound of brown dirt, stood in stark contrast to the green grass all around.

A tombstone marked her grave now. It hadn't been there the day of the funeral. Auntie Geraldine must have arranged it. Sparrow leaned close to read the words etched in stone. *Lilly Dalton, Beloved Daughter, Devoted Sister, Loving Mother, Sweet Soul Taken Too Soon.*

It seemed perfect and too simple at the same time. It summed up Mama's traits, but in life, she encompassed so much more than those lines implied. The words didn't capture the warmth and safety Sparrow felt when wrapped in one of her hugs or the sound of her voice when she sang along to the country hymns that played on the radio while she cooked.

She wished she'd known they were running this way. She would have brought Mama flowers for her grave.

"That's real nice," Johnny said quietly.

Sparrow nodded, biting her lip to keep the tears from falling. She sometimes worried that if she cried she'd make it harder for Mama to come back, as if crying for her cemented her fate, and Sparrow refused to be the lock that barred the door. "I guess it is."

Sparrow sat down on the grass.

Johnny sat next to her. "My uncle Mason's eyes have been red-rimmed all week."

"Why?" Sparrow asked, surprised.

"Because of your mama. I bet you didn't know they were good friends when they were kids. They even dated for a time."

"No, I didn't," Sparrow said, genuinely taken aback by this news. She couldn't imagine it. She'd never heard of Castos and Daltons being friends. Auntie Geraldine hated the Castos almost as much as she hated Dalton House. If friendship between Castos and Daltons sounded like stretched truth, then dating sounded like a tall tale. As far as Castos went, Mason stood a cut above the rest, but it didn't change the fact that Casto blood colored his veins. In Beulah, family name rose above all else, like salt froth on a wave.

"Yep, they did. According to Uncle Mason, they fell in love at the flea market while digging through a box of old gospel records."

"My mama adored hymns." Sparrow envisioned a younger Mama falling in love because of music. She could imagine it. "How long ago was this?"

"Not sure exactly. Before all of us, but I think it's why he had this." Johnny reached into his back pocket and pulled out a faded picture. He handed it to Sparrow.

The picture was of Mama. She looked a lot younger and almost too different to recognize, but Sparrow could still see the hints of the familiar features that would age into the face she knew so well.

In the photograph, Mama leaned against an old pickup truck at the flea market. She flipped the picture over. An inscription on the back read *Love never says goodbye*.

"Maeve and I felt real bad about the other day. When we saw this, we thought you might like to have it."

"Thanks," Sparrow whispered. It was the nicest thing anyone had done for her since Mama died. The Castos were full of surprises. "Will your uncle miss it?"

Johnny shrugged. "Probably. But there are so many kids running around our house no one can keep nothing safe. He won't know we took it to give to you."

"Thanks." Sparrow felt grateful to have this hint at a part of Mama's life she didn't know anything about.

"Um . . . there's something else," Johnny said, a bit nervous. "You really don't know who your daddy is, right?"

She shook her head. "No, I don't."

"You don't believe all that bunk about your daddy being the swamp, do ya?"

Sparrow didn't know what she believed. Sometimes she wondered if it could be true. After all, her only friend was a ghost. Her father might as well be the swamp. She didn't share these thoughts with Johnny, though. Beulah considered her strange enough already. If she confessed she sometimes wondered if Mama had conjured her from the very swamp itself, they'd lock her up.

"No. Mama didn't like to talk about it, so I didn't pry. It didn't seem right somehow. People were always whispering behind her back. I wanted to be on her side. Besides, I didn't need a daddy. I had Mama."

Johnny nodded solemnly. She could tell he knew all about sticking by family when the town ganged up against them. "Maeve and I were talking. You know how my uncle has been pretty torn up about your mama dying and everything?"

"Yeah, you said."

"Well, he left town about ten years ago."

"Sure. Everyone knows that." Sparrow watched a thin mist swirl around Johnny, glide away, and then come back again. The spirits seemed to like him.

"Well . . ."

"Tell her already." Both Sparrow and Johnny jumped at the sound of Maeve's voice behind them.

They twisted around to look at Maeve. Aside from her eyeliner smeared into black streaks below her eyes and her red hair darkened by sweat, she looked no worse for wear. Sparrow guessed she'd outrun Ansley and then doubled back to find them.

Maeve smacked her brother on the head. "Way to keep up your guard. If I'd been Andrew, I'd have caught you and given you a thrashing before you realized what happened."

"Tell me what?" Sparrow asked.

Maeve plopped down beside her brother and the spirits surrounding him scattered like a flock of birds. "We think our uncle Mason is your daddy."

"*What?*" For a moment, the world tilted. Maeve's crazy proclamation made Sparrow feel like everything she thought she knew had been thrown off-kilter. All the words Beulah called the Castos behind their backs, but she had never believed, came to Sparrow—cheats, good-for-nothings, *liars*. Sparrow narrowed her eyes suspiciously at Maeve. "Why do you think that?"

"Because"—Maeve started counting things out on her fingers—"he left about ten years ago, before you were born, he came back when your mama got sick, and he's been crying over her ever since."

It was true, Mason had only recently moved back to Beulah. The town gossips said he'd left to seek his fortune in the oil business. Now he worked at the local 76 station.

Sparrow didn't know if he'd made his fortune or not, but she doubted it. She wouldn't work at Beulah's one-pump gas station if she had a fortune sitting in the bank.

"Those are a bunch of coincidences." Sparrow looked less like a Casto than she did a Dalton.

"Yeah, but he had the picture." Maeve pointed to the photograph in Sparrow's hand. "Did you read the back?"

Sparrow flipped the picture over. *"Love never says good-bye,"* she said, reading the inscription out loud.

"That's right. We think because your mama was a Dalton and Uncle Mason a Casto . . . you know that wasn't goin' to go over well. We think he left Beulah because he wanted to prove himself worthy of marrying a Dalton. If he made a lot of money and became a rich Casto . . . well, there's no shame in marrying rich, is there? Casto or no."

"Seems far-fetched. Why would it be such a big secret that my own mama wouldn't tell me?" Sparrow didn't like the idea that Mama might have kept this secret from her. If Mason Casto *was* her daddy, then she should be the one telling Maeve and Johnny the truth about him, not the other way around.

"Pretty, perfect Lilly Dalton falling in love with a Casto? You think your family would ever want the town to know about that?" Maeve crossed her arms in a challenge.

Sparrow wanted to deny it, but Maeve spoke the truth. Daltons didn't marry Castos in Beulah. Marrying a rich Casto might even be a stretch.

"I don't look like a Casto." Sparrow put her tanned arm next to Maeve's sun-scorched one. During the summer months, Maeve's skin flamed an angry red as if whipped, while Sparrow's olive complexion simply deepened.

Maeve looked at Sparrow like she was the dumbest kid in the world. "How do you know what a Casto-Dalton kid would look like? There's never been one."

Sparrow supposed Maeve had a point. Sometimes kids looked like their folks. Sometimes they didn't. She mulled it over for a few minutes. Did she want a daddy bad enough to go looking for him at the Castos'? She'd been so firmly planted on Mama's side that even the idea of a daddy seemed disloyal. Now, though, having a daddy might solve some issues that were turning out to be big problems. If she had a daddy, that would mean she wouldn't have to go to Havisham with Auntie Geraldine. She could live with him instead, and a Beulah-born daddy would be super convenient, as she wouldn't have to leave Beulah. She'd been trying not to think about it because the idea of leaving Dalton House made Sparrow feel sick.

As she thought on it, she realized convenience and problem solving didn't rank as the only benefits. A daddy would love her. Sparrow had been feeling so lonely and heartsick that the idea took root like beggarweed. "You think I should ask him?"

"NO!" Maeve and Johnny shouted together.

"We'd both be scrubbing oil off the floor of the 76 station if he found out we'd been pokin' around in his business," Johnny said.

"Or worse," Maeve added. "Besides, even though we're sure, you need more proof first. You don't want to have to *ask* him if you're his daughter, you want to be able to *tell* him you are."

Sparrow drew the picture close and ran her finger over Mama's face. Maeve sounded like she was scheming, but she made a good point. It would be better for Sparrow to have definitive proof. "Where do I find proof?"

"Lucky for you, we have a plan." Maeve elbowed her brother in the ribs. "Isn't that right, Johnny?"

Johnny nodded enthusiastically. "We sure do."

Sparrow sized up the Castos. She wondered if their plan was a good one.

CHAPTER EIGHT

There is nothing like the blackness of a moonless country night, so dark and thick it feels almost solid. Sparrow felt as if she could reach out and push the darkness aside, like a swimmer moving through water, but she couldn't be bothered. Instead, she closed her eyes and drifted on the porch swing, one foot cast overboard, a rudder to guide her gentle swaying.

Exhaustion made Sparrow's body heavy with weariness, but her mind whirled with the promise of a message from Mama, and Maeve and Johnny's revelation. Despite lingering doubts, the suggestion that Mason was her father and that he lived down the road at the Casto place appealed to Sparrow.

She pushed the swing with her foot, and it rocked obediently.

It *was* possible, she supposed.

If Mason Casto were her father, it would explain a lot. Like why Mama had kept it secret and why he had Mama's picture after all those years.

She wouldn't mind having Mason Casto for a father. He worked hard at the 76 station, and she didn't think he'd ever spent time in jail like some of the Casto men. Plus, if what Maeve and Johnny said was true, he'd loved Mama so much he'd left his family and Beulah to seek his fortune so he could come back and marry her. When she looked at it in that light, he seemed heroic. Besides, she'd rather be related to a Casto than Auntie Geraldine.

When Maeve and Johnny first told Sparrow, she felt hurt that Mama had kept the truth from her, but Sparrow had spent the afternoon and most of the evening thinking it through. She reckoned if the story was true, Mama had meant for Sparrow to know. Only she'd run out of time to tell her. Sparrow figured Mama had kept the secret about her daddy all this time because she wanted to tell Sparrow about Mason with him by her side, but he had gotten back to Beulah too late. By the time Mason returned, Mama was really sick and Auntie Geraldine was in charge. Auntie Geraldine hated Castos. She'd never let Sparrow be related to one.

The more Sparrow thought on it, the more she liked her theory. Believing that Mama had intended to tell her about Mason, but that she had run out of time, not only absolved Mama, it absolved Sparrow.

At first, Sparrow felt guilty for wanting a daddy now that Mama was gone, but Sparrow didn't want to replace Mama with Mason. She wanted to replace Auntie Geraldine, and that wasn't disloyal to Mama. That was survival.

Maeve and Johnny claimed they had a plan to get the proof Sparrow needed, but they wouldn't tell Sparrow what it was or how long it would take. Sparrow didn't possess the patience to wait for Maeve and Johnny. She had her own plan. She intended to ask the one person in Beulah who *knew all* and *saw all*—the fortune-teller.

But that wasn't the only reason Sparrow was going back to Elena, or the most important. Sparrow wanted Mama's message.

The only thing that stood between Sparrow and everything she wanted to know was the twenty dollars she needed for a proper reading. Unfortunately, Sparrow didn't have two cents to rub together, and Auntie Geraldine was as stingy as a miser.

At the sound of car wheels crunching gravel on the drive, Sparrow sat up.

When she'd gotten home, Auntie Geraldine had not been there. At first, this hadn't troubled Sparrow. She was a country kid. From sunup to sundown, she spent her time outdoors. Most days she left Dalton House early in the morning and returned only when her stomach told her to come home for meals. Yet while she was accustomed to these freedoms, she wasn't used to an empty house at night.

This had been a new experience for her, and she'd found it lonely.

Auntie Geraldine climbed the porch steps, and Sparrow rushed to open the screen door for her. Sparrow felt disappointed in Auntie Geraldine. It was her job to take care of Sparrow, and she wasn't doing it well. Sparrow still hadn't had dinner and her stomach rumbled like a rolling boulder, reminding her she had missed lunch too. Before Auntie Geraldine could walk through the door, Sparrow said, "Where have you been? I've been waiting here for hours."

Auntie Geraldine paused on the third step, and the two Daltons stood eye to eye.

"Where have *I been*?" Auntie Geraldine asked with a slippery tone.

"Yes," Sparrow said cautiously. Her brow furrowed, and then she remembered.

She was supposed to wait for Auntie Geraldine at Long's. So much had happened since then, she'd forgotten all about it.

"I think the question is, where have *you* been?" Auntie Geraldine said tersely, and continued climbing the steps.

"I've been here." Sparrow stepped aside to let Auntie Geraldine pass.

"Well, that's perfect. You've been here lazing about while I've been all over town looking for you. Driving up and down the highway. Wondering if the marsh had swallowed you whole." The pitch of Auntie Geraldine's voice rose with each word. "Then about an hour ago, I heard someone saw you running around with Maeve and Johnny Casto, so I drove out to their place. They said you'd walked home hours ago!"

"Something happened at Long's, and I couldn't wait there."

"Yes, I heard all about it from Ansley and Andrew Monroe." Auntie Geraldine waved her hand dismissively. "Those Castos were causing trouble, and you were right in the mix. *Again.*"

"That's not true."

"Isn't it?"

It wasn't, but Sparrow hesitated, unsure of how to answer. She didn't want to rat on Andrew and Ansley even if they were at fault. At the same time, she wanted to defend Maeve and Johnny. Her newly formed loyalty to Maeve and Johnny won.

"Ansley and Andrew started it. We were running away from them, not fighting."

Auntie Geraldine rolled her eyes. "Castos running instead of fighting? I'll believe that when pigs fly. You stay far away from those troublemakers, you hear me?"

Auntie Geraldine didn't understand. Maeve and Johnny weren't troublemakers. They were something else altogether. Johnny had stuck up for Sparrow at the funeral, they'd given her Mama's picture, and they'd told her about Mason Casto. In those three small acts, they'd become something Sparrow had never had before—friends.

"I like the Castos."

"You would." Auntie Geraldine had pulled her hair back into a low bun, but it no longer looked tidy. Pieces were falling out, and it gave her a wild look.

Sparrow felt bad that Auntie Geraldine had spent the evening searching for her, but she also didn't understand why Auntie Geraldine hadn't checked at the house. She didn't blame Auntie Geraldine exactly, but it did seem uncharacteristically inefficient. Sparrow opened her mouth to say this, but Auntie Geraldine cut her off.

"Look here. I've had about as much of your nonsense as I can take. You will *not*, under any circumstance, go into town again. Do you understand?"

"You can't stop me from going to town. Besides, you took me there." Sparrow would rather polish silverware during a lightning storm than be trapped at home all day with Auntie Geraldine.

"Yes, I can. And I told you to stay put at Long's until

I came back for you. You deliberately disobeyed me." Auntie Geraldine glared at Sparrow and Sparrow tried not to fidget under her fierce gaze. She felt like an onion being peeled. Now that it was only the two of them, Auntie Geraldine had the power to do whatever she wanted to Sparrow.

The seconds seemed to tick by like minutes, and Sparrow, uncomfortable, shifted her weight. She wanted to get as far away from Auntie Geraldine as she could before things got worse. She looked at the front door longingly.

The Boy was there. He stood next to the door, watching them. He always looked the same. Round cherub cheeks and dark hair cut close, a white dress shirt unbuttoned at the neck and cuffs, black pants a tad too short, and black boots unlaced, with the tongues flapping.

When she looked his way, his lips curved at the edges mischievously.

Sparrow shook her head imperceptibly. Auntie Geraldine seemed to be simmering just below her boiling point. She was like a teakettle ready to blow, and Sparrow didn't need the Boy turning up the heat.

The Boy winked at Sparrow and moved away from the wall.

Sparrow scowled at him, frustrated at his free will. The Boy did what he wanted, and he seemed to want to vex Auntie Geraldine as much as possible now that she lived at Dalton

House again. While Sparrow understood the compulsion, it complicated life with Auntie Geraldine. Like poking a snake with a stick, it riled her up and made her mean.

Mama had not been immune from the Boy's pranks, but he'd been playful and less obvious with her. He'd teased her in more explainable ways—lights going on and off for no reason, unexpected loud noises, items that went missing and later reappeared in odd places, and Mama mostly rationalized them as such. When the lights flickered, she'd sigh and complain about old wiring. Loud noises inspired comments about creaky floorboards and the house's need to settle. Lost items were simply laughed off as absentmindedness.

The exception had been the day the saltshaker slid slowly across the table for no apparent reason. On that day, Mama's face had turned ashen, and she'd whisked Sparrow outside into the sunshine. They'd explored the marsh until Mama's color returned. Of course, the Boy had spent that afternoon with them, but he seemed to feel bad for scaring Mama, and only Sparrow had known that the Boy trailed them like a repentant puppy. He'd been more careful around Mama after that, but his relationship with Auntie Geraldine seemed to be moving in the opposite direction. He seemed to want her attention.

The Boy strode leisurely across the porch toward the screen door, stomping loudly as he went. The noise filled the silence, like the dreaded sound of a shotgun blast on the first day of hunting season.

Sparrow glanced at Auntie Geraldine, trying to gauge her response. Auntie Geraldine watched Sparrow, her face as impassive as if she were considering her grocery list. Just as Sparrow started to wonder if Auntie Geraldine could actually hear the Boy's stomping, he reached the screen door.

He threw it open. The door flew back, straining its hinges. Then the old, rusted springs kicked in and the door swung back toward the frame, slamming closed.

Auntie Geraldine's blue eyes shifted to the door.

The Boy threw the door open again. Again, it swung open as wide as its springs would allow, and then slammed shut.

Sparrow wanted to throttle him.

The Boy drew the door open a third time.

Sparrow studied Auntie Geraldine's profile. What Auntie Geraldine saw, Sparrow couldn't be sure, but she could imagine that watching the door open and close without cause on a windless night would be terrifying. A sight like that would scare the wits out of most people. Auntie Geraldine didn't even flinch.

Before the Boy could let go of the door again, Auntie Geraldine turned away from it to Sparrow. She considered Sparrow, her lips pulling into a tight, disapproving line. She stayed like that for a moment and then did something unexpected and brilliant. She dropped her car keys into her pocketbook and snapped it closed.

"Good night, Sparrow," she said evenly, and walked into the house, ignoring the Boy altogether.

"Good night," Sparrow murmured.

The Boy deflated. He let the door bang close one last time, but didn't reach for it again.

Lights flicked on inside the house as Auntie Geraldine made her way from room to room, lighting it up like a Christmas tree.

Sparrow stood in the center of the porch, too stunned to move.

If Auntie Geraldine had gotten more than she'd bargained for in Sparrow, Sparrow had certainly gotten more than she'd bargained for in Auntie Geraldine.

CHAPTER NINE

Sunday-morning service was a timeworn Beulah ritual as old as the marsh. Everyone in town went to church. They didn't all go to the same church, but they all went. Sparrow wanted to skip it since it was her first Sunday without Mama and it felt too sad, but Auntie Geraldine flat-out refused to consider the idea. When Sparrow reminded Auntie Geraldine she had forbidden Sparrow to go to town under *any circumstance*, Auntie Geraldine seemed to come undone. She turned as red as a beet and recited all of Sparrow's faults in a voice so loud that even after she finished yelling, Sparrow's ears continued to ring. They were halfway to church before Sparrow's hearing returned to normal.

By the time they got to church, the preacher already stood in front of the big red doors, greeting parishioners. Auntie Geraldine ascended the church steps like an honored guest and waited to be acknowledged.

"Geraldine, nice to have you in town for a while. How are you holding up?" He laid a hand on her shoulder and gazed at her with rheumy eyes.

"We're managing. It's difficult, of course." She gazed back at him, her expression conveying the appropriate emotion for a grieving sister.

"You're in our prayers," he said, his voice solemn.

"Thank you so much," Auntie Geraldine whispered before walking on.

As Sparrow walked by, the preacher nodded to her but didn't say anything. Sparrow hadn't seen him since Mama's funeral and she wondered if he might be mad at her for refusing to take part in the service, but then thought maybe he didn't greet the kids. Even though Sparrow went to church every Sunday, she wasn't familiar with this part of the weekly ritual because she and Mama always got to church late. On Sunday mornings, they would slip into the back pew as the congregation sang the final note of the first hymn.

Curious, Sparrow paused to watch the preacher greet the rest of the folks. The next in line were the Monroes. Wesley Monroe stepped up and offered his hand to the preacher.

"Wesley," the preacher said. "Nice to see you. Oh, and Ansley, don't you look a picture."

Ansley beamed at him and did a half spin in her white dress. "Thank you. It's new."

"Well, it suits you," he said, and then turned to Andrew. "That's quite a shiner you have there." He pressed his pudgy fingers to the yellowing bruise.

Andrew leaned back, pulling his face out of poking distance. "Yes, sir," he said. He looked away as if embarrassed.

Wesley put his hand on Andrew's shoulder. "Scuffle with the Castos. You know how those kids are."

"They're often in my prayers," the preacher said. "But as Methodists, they are out of my jurisdiction. Each shepherd must lead his flock the way he sees fit." He sighed heavily, making it clear he did not think the Methodist minister was doing a good job of leading his flock.

"Sparrow," Auntie Geraldine hissed.

Sparrow jumped like a startled jackrabbit. *"What?"*

"Stop staring. It's rude. Come with me."

Sparrow tore her gaze away from the preacher and the Monroes, and followed Auntie Geraldine to the front of the church. Auntie Geraldine ushered Sparrow into the second pew. It was packed, but Auntie Geraldine impatiently waved her in anyway and Sparrow complied, forcing everyone already seated to move down.

The preacher entered the church, and services were officially under way.

76

Sparrow did her best to stay focused, but after ten minutes her eyes felt droopy and her limbs heavy. The preacher's honey voice combined with the summer heat soothed her like a lullaby. She started to slump to the side and Auntie Geraldine jabbed her in the ribs.

Sparrow jerked to attention and crossed her arms. She wished she sat next to Mama instead of Auntie Geraldine. Mama always let Sparrow rest her head on her shoulder when the preacher got long-winded and the heat of so many bodies crammed together made the nave feel like a steaming shower.

Simply remembering Mama in the familiar setting made Sparrow's eyes prick with tears and her throat tighten. Mama had not sent a message yet, but Sparrow had not given up hope. She had faith in Mama.

Sparrow did her best to focus on the preacher's words instead of Mama, but the heat made it near impossible to concentrate, and after a few minutes she inched down the backrest so she could lean her head against it.

Auntie Geraldine shot Sparrow a look, but Sparrow pretended she didn't notice. The only good part about going to church with Auntie Geraldine was that she couldn't yell at her for that hour. Not even Auntie Geraldine had enough nerve to disrupt Sunday service.

Sparrow was starting to nod off again when the Boy slipped into the space between her and the woman beside her. Like a mouse sliding under a door, he wedged himself between them, arms and legs pulled in close to fit into the small gap.

Sparrow scooted toward Auntie Geraldine to give him more room, but Auntie Geraldine's lips pulled tight and her eyes got mean. She didn't need words to tell Sparrow to stop squirming.

Sparrow watched the Boy from the corner of her eye and noticed him start to spread out slowly, like a pitcher filling with water.

The more the Boy stretched out, the more uncomfortable the woman next to him seemed to get, as if the space next to her suddenly swarmed with bees. When his ghostly arm touched hers, she slapped it as if she'd been stung.

Auntie Geraldine gave Sparrow a withering look.

Sparrow bulged her eyes back at Auntie Geraldine to show she had nothing to do with the woman's discomfort.

The preacher got distracted by the commotion in their row and lost his place in his notes. He accidently referred to Jesus as the devil and started to sweat. He pulled out his hanky and mopped the bald part of his head where it was wettest. He flipped through his notes, but struggled to find his spot.

Auntie Geraldine pursed her lips and narrowed her eyes in an expression that clearly said *knock it off.*

Sparrow shrugged, trying to tell Auntie Geraldine she didn't know why she was blaming her.

The Boy spread out a bit more, and the woman huffed. She shoved over, causing a chain reaction all the way down the pew.

The preacher dropped his notes and they floated to the floor like giant snowflakes. As he bent down to gather them, his robe hitched up, revealing black dress socks and bare legs.

A snicker went through the congregation.

Sparrow had never considered what was beneath the pastor's robes before, but now that she'd had a glimpse, she hoped he wore something else besides socks.

Clearly flustered, the pastor stacked his notes on the pulpit and continued his sermon. Only he seemed to have completely forgotten where he left off and started at the beginning again.

Sparrow sighed, and resigned herself to an extra long homily.

Now that the Boy was settled, he sat as polite as an acolyte and listened to the bumbled sermon with an air of benevolent patience.

Sparrow chanced a glance at Auntie Geraldine and felt certain she was not granting the preacher the same understanding. Sparrow knew Auntie Geraldine expected everyone, even the preacher, to live up to his responsibilities. Blowing the eleven o'clock Sunday service was unforgivable in her eyes.

When the service ended thirty minutes later than usual, the congregation stampeded out of the building like a drove of pigs.

Before Auntie Geraldine had a chance to reprimand Sparrow about her church behavior, one of the Sunshine Ladies cornered Auntie Geraldine and asked her to help at the annual charity barbecue. With the service running long, the Sunshine Ladies were severely behind schedule and aflutter with excitement. Mr. Monroe had donated several copies of the book he wrote to help raise money. He planned to do a book signing and give a short speech. The Sunshine Ladies were loath to put on a bad showing by being unprepared.

Auntie Geraldine went off to help and Sparrow skedaddled in the opposite direction, and the Boy trailed her faithfully.

She found a shady spot under a big oak and sat. The Boy positioned himself beside her, settling in a way that reminded Sparrow of a cat. He languorously stretched out as if he ruled the grass and everything before him.

When the church bells rang the hour, Sparrow saw some of the Castos walking down Main Street. All the Casto kids slurped on Popsicles from the Superette. Sparrow saw Mason Casto rub Johnny on the head and Johnny beam up at him. It made her wonder if Mason had been the one to buy all those treats. She decided he had and that he was a good guy.

The news Maeve and Johnny had shared with Sparrow about Mason Casto came flooding back, and her mind started churning again. Walking down Main Street eating a Popsicle on a hot Sunday looked like heaven to her, and she wondered what it felt like to be part of that big family.

As if they'd been waiting for the perfect moment to harass Sparrow, Ansley and Andrew sauntered up, carrying copies of their father's book, *Orphan Trains: Small Towns, Big Hearts*.

"All alone, swamp rat? What happened to your new best friends? Are you too weird even for Castaways?" Ansley pointed to Main Street. The Casto clan was almost out of sight, but not quite.

Sparrow sighed. She wished she were walking home with the Castos. Even from behind they looked happy. Mason Casto had his arm draped over Johnny's shoulder, and next to them, Maeve skipped down the road.

"You know they go to the Methodist church," Sparrow said, giving an explanation for why she wasn't with them even though no one expected her to be on a Casto family outing.

"That's right. Flounder's Church," Ansley quipped. Their church name was Foundry, not Flounder's, as Ansley knew. Her nicknames were getting tiresome.

"Can't you leave them alone?" Sparrow asked.

"No, I can't. Look at his face." Ansley pointed to Andrew's eye, which, while still tinged yellow, was healing. "That's the third one this month. I'm going to make Maeve pay for what she did. You too, since you love the Castaways so much. Unless you want to help *us*."

"I'm siding with them." Sparrow stood up, even though she felt a little shaky. She didn't like the odds— two against one.

Andrew thrust his face toward Sparrow. "Look at my eye." He pointed at the bruise. Up close, Sparrow noticed a tint of green, the color of algae. "And you blame me?"

The Boy rose too. He looked from Ansley and Andrew to Sparrow. He seemed to be reading the situation, trying to gauge the tension.

"You're the one who cheated," Sparrow said.

Andrew's face turned Popsicle red. He looked like he wanted to throttle Sparrow.

Ansley put her arm across her brother's chest as if to keep him from acting on his impulse. "You know you're an orphan now."

"Am not."

"Of course you are," Ansley explained sweetly, as if talking to a toddler. "Your mother's dead and you don't have a father. So, orphan."

"I have a family."

"An aunt who doesn't want you. That makes you an orphan."

The label felt like a jolt.

Ansley poked Sparrow. "Orphan."

The Boy moved in front of Sparrow protectively. He seemed to expand, pulling himself vertically so that he became a barrier between her and Ansley. The new shape thinned him and he looked slightly less solid and more opaque.

Sparrow had never seen him do anything like it before.

Ansley's condescending expression shifted to alarm. She rubbed her eyes and backed up. "She's blurry. I can't see!"

"What?" Andrew asked.

"She did something. I can't see!" Ansley yelled, slightly hysterical.

Andrew gaped at Sparrow. He looked terrified.

"What's wrong with you two?" Sparrow asked.

"Freak!" Ansley yelled. She grabbed her brother by the arm and dragged him behind her as she ran.

As Sparrow watched Andrew and Ansley race toward their father, the Boy lost volume, returning to his usual shape like a deflating balloon. He reclaimed his spot on the grass and winked at Sparrow. He seemed very pleased with himself.

She smiled back, perplexed but grateful. She didn't know what the twins thought they saw, or what the Boy had done exactly, but whatever he'd done, it had scared them away. She might not have too many people on her side, but at least she had him.

As Sparrow settled next to the Boy, she tried to muster up happiness at the twins' defeat, but she couldn't help feeling like the loser. *Orphan* bounced around her brain like an echo. Up until Ansley uttered the word, she considered herself beloved daughter of Lilly Dalton even though Mama lingered out of reach on the other side. But now she realized Beulah saw her differently. Worse, she saw herself differently.

Sparrow didn't want to be an orphan and she didn't have to be. She had a father. She just needed the proof to claim him.

CHAPTER TEN

Sparrow sat at the kitchen table, as prim as a princess, with the newest edition of the *Herald* spread before her.

Beulah only printed one paper per month, and even with that infrequency, the editor, Miss Ruby, often had trouble filling up more than three pages. No one thought it odd that Miss Ruby owned the drugstore and also owned the paper. Miss Ruby was a shrewd businesswoman. Only Wesley Monroe rivaled Miss Ruby when it came to success. Miss Ruby had started buying up businesses as a young woman. Now, aged to perfection, she claimed several grandchildren and owned numerous businesses in Beulah as well as Havisham, so it made sense that she owned the newspaper.

On the front page of this month's edition, a gritty black-and-white photograph of Miss Ruby with her arm around the fortune-teller took up the top half of the paper. Underneath the photo, Miss Ruby recounted her experience with the child psychic. According to the article, Miss Ruby had been astounded and at one point flabbergasted by the accuracy of the girl's knowledge of her life heretofore, making Miss Ruby convinced that the fortune-teller's predictions for the future were as good as verified already.

Sparrow read Miss Ruby's account for the fifth time. She needed to get back to that fortune-teller. If anyone could answer Sparrow's questions about Mama and her father, it was Elena, the child psychic, and there was something almost magical about having the newspaper article delivered to her front door. It made it feel like a summons.

The problem was Auntie Geraldine.

She had forbidden Sparrow to go to town. Though she'd made an exception for church, Sparrow didn't think that dispensation covered going to the flea market to consult with a psychic. That's why Sparrow sat at the table so primly. She was biding her time and trying to look like the picture of obedience. Auntie Geraldine couldn't keep her hawk eyes on Sparrow all day.

Auntie Geraldine paced about the kitchen while she talked on the phone to Mr. Monroe. From the depth of Auntie Geraldine's sighs and the curtness of her one-word answers, Sparrow assumed that Mr. Monroe had nothing to say that pleased Auntie Geraldine. With a final exasperated sigh, Auntie Geraldine hung up the phone.

"He needs me to go to his office. Today. Honestly, you'd think the man had never settled an estate before. Not that anyone would call this creepy old shack an estate. But you know what I mean." Auntie Geraldine waved her hand dismissively.

Sparrow didn't know what Auntie Geraldine meant at all. In her opinion, Dalton House was the grandest place in Beulah. Normally, Sparrow would have told Auntie Geraldine as much, but she held her tongue. She needed Auntie Geraldine to let her guard down so she could put her plans in action.

"I'll have to drive over there."

"Okay," Sparrow said as blandly as possible, which took quite a bit of effort. Auntie Geraldine wore a red dress. Sparrow had never seen her in any color other than black or navy. The contrast of the bright scarlet against her alabaster skin was alarming. Something about the color red on Auntie Geraldine reminded Sparrow of holly berries—the poisonous ones.

Auntie Geraldine inspected Sparrow. "Why are you acting so . . . docile? It's not like you."

Sparrow resisted the urge to roll her eyes. She thought this was the way Auntie Geraldine wanted her to act. She couldn't win. "Just a little tired, I suppose."

"Hmm . . ." Auntie Geraldine seemed reluctant to trust Sparrow. "I'll know if you go to town."

"I won't." Sparrow intended to visit the flea market, not town.

"I don't like it. Leaving you here unsupervised. You're sure to get up to something, but I don't see that I have much choice. You mark my words, though. One foot out of place and I'll give this house away to the first person who walks by, and we'll be in Havisham by week's end."

Something about the way Auntie Geraldine said it made Sparrow feel cold. Auntie Geraldine meant it. She wanted to leave Dalton House and Beulah so badly that she'd use any excuse to dump it. She probably would have sold the house right out from under Mama, deathbed and all, if Mr. Monroe hadn't been holding her up. Apparently, the law had a lot to say about inheritances. None of which Auntie Geraldine found to her liking. It was only a matter of time before Auntie Geraldine browbeat Mr. Monroe into letting her sell the house.

Sparrow pulled the newspaper to her like a talisman. She needed to talk to Elena again. Sparrow had been waiting for Mama's message to be revealed or for Mama to come to her, but Mama remained stubbornly taciturn. If Mama wouldn't come to Sparrow, Sparrow would find a way to cross the divide that separated them.

As soon as Sparrow heard Auntie Geraldine's car tires on the gravel drive, she began to search the house. She needed a way to pay for her next visit to Elena, and the watch vendor at the flea market had given her an idea.

Sparrow remembered seeing an old pocket watch that no one wanted anymore. Over the years, it had gotten moved from drawer to drawer without much interest or care whenever Mama thought it was in the way, so Sparrow figured it was okay to sell it. There were castoffs all over Dalton House. Things had a tendency to pile up when generation after generation lived in the same house. Sparrow probably wouldn't get much money in exchange for the watch, but it had to be worth twenty dollars at least. Last time she'd seen it, it still worked.

The Boy had been scarcer than a Florida panther all morning, but now he watched her curiously as she rummaged through every drawer in the hickory desk. She finally found the brass watch in the back of the bottom drawer.

Triumphant, she showed it to the Boy.

The Boy cocked his head inquisitively and then reached his ghostly hand toward the watch.

Unsure of his intentions, she closed her fingers around it. The Boy was a prankster, and she didn't always trust him.

Sparrow turned the watch crown and held it to her ear. She was delighted to hear the rhythmic ticking. She tucked the watch into the back pocket of her cutoffs and started to leave.

She paused at the door to see if the Boy followed her. He seemed unaware that she was leaving. He stared at the hickory desk as if mesmerized. *Spirits*, Sparrow thought, and walked out the door, leaving the Boy behind.

She went down to the marsh and then walked along the water's edge, following the path to town. It took longer to walk that way, but she was less likely to be seen.

Little bugs skittered and bounced before her, disturbed by her passing. She smiled at their jittery movement. The marsh buzzed in the morning hours. Its inhabitants liked to take full advantage of the cooler moments. By the time the noonday sun commanded the sky, the heat would be insufferable and the wetland creatures would burrow deep into the mire to stay cool.

For the moment, the marsh idled at low tide, and the mud flats and the sandbar were visible. Folks said the sandbar ran the length of the marsh. Supposedly, it connected Beulah to the sea, making it possible to walk its entire length. Sparrow longed to try it, but no kid in Beulah heard the tale of the sandbar without the warnings that went with it. The marsh continually shifted, its form ever-changing. The moon pulled at its tides, and Beulah's frequent, sudden rains could fill its banks to bursting. A sandbar, no matter how vast, risked being quickly overrun by the water that flanked it, and anyone on it would be trapped.

A snowy egret took slow, graceful steps through the marsh, and Sparrow wondered what it would be like to traverse that watery landscape. One day, she'd attempt it, warnings be hanged.

She followed the marsh to the road and the road to Main Street. Once on Main Street, the flea market quickly came into view. She had not been fibbing to Auntie Geraldine when she said she wouldn't go *into* town, since the flea market had been erected on the border of town near the 76 station. Town officially started two blocks down from the one-pump gas station.

Sparrow heard the sound of an automobile coming down the road. She ducked into the scrub brush that flanked the road to stay out of sight of the oncoming car. She didn't dare risk an accidental run-in with Auntie Geraldine. Sound traveled far and fast on Beulah's flat roads, and a minute ticked by before the truck creating the noise came into view.

When it got close enough, Sparrow recognized Mason Casto's truck.

The 76 station sat directly across the street from Sparrow's hiding place, and she watched Mason pull in, park, and hop out. He used a huge ring of keys to unlock the garage doors, and he rolled them up. He stepped into coveralls and started to work on an old car.

Sparrow observed him closely, searching for clues of their kinship. Already, it burned hotter than blue blazes, and his red hair hung heavy with sweat. The moisture made it look darker than usual, and summer had sun-baked his skin to a deep brown. Gazing at him from afar, she felt his coloring resembled her own. While she liked the romanticism of Mama conjuring her from the very swamp itself, she had to admit that a real, live Beulah-born daddy would be more useful than a mystical one. Sparrow had to have someone on her side that other people could see. Besides, without a daddy, Sparrow really was an orphan—a moniker too sad to bear.

Then there was the other feeling. The idea of a daddy to love her enticed Sparrow the way sugar lured ants. Simply thinking about it warmed the cold place that had taken up residence in the pit of her stomach since Mama got sick.

Sparrow had quite a bit to sort out, but that was the reason she had to talk to Elena again. She emerged from her hiding place and continued on to the flea market. She made her way to the periwinkle van. When it came into sight, she just about fainted.

It seemed like the entire town waited in line for the fortune-teller.

CHAPTER ELEVEN

Sparrow found the crowd waiting in line for Elena astonishing considering most folks in Beulah knew their future just by glancing back a generation.

She surveyed the crowd. Folks lingered by the antiquities table or stood in line chatting. The wait looked to be an hour at least. Maybe Beulah wished for change more than she thought.

Sparrow spied Clara Casto, one of Maeve and Johnny's older sisters, standing at the end of the line and took her place behind Clara. "Are you waiting to have your fortune told?"

"I wouldn't pass this opportunity by if I had to make a deal with the devil," Clara said. "Which I practically had to do. I borrowed money from Maeve. That girl is a scrooge. Saves every penny and then doles it out like a loan shark. Charges interest and everything. But it's going to be worth it. Did you read Miss Ruby's article?"

"Five times."

Clara pointed to herself. "Seven. I'm applying to Vanderbilt in the fall. I want to know if I'm going to get in."

Sparrow did her best to suppress her astonishment at the idea of a Casto applying to a prestigious college. The Castos had a reputation for making trouble, not grades. Every time she spoke to a Casto, they surprised her. "What do you want to study?"

"Medicine." Clara's tone held a touch of challenge. It dared Sparrow to make a snide comment. The Monroes would, but not Sparrow. She was impressed by Clara's noble goals.

"You think you could hold my place here?" Sparrow asked.

"I don't know." Clara hitched her thumbs into the back pockets of her shorts. "Been pretty busy and it's like an oven out here. People don't like waiting in line, especially in heat like this. Might be hard to hold your spot."

"I won't be but a second. I just need to run over to that watch guy." Sparrow pointed in the direction of the vendor with the broken pocket watch. "If someone comes, holler and I'll run back over."

"Come right back if you hear me yell for you."

"Promise." Sparrow took off toward the watch vendor, her flip-flops slapping against the bottom of her feet.

When she got to the portly vendor, she pulled out the brass pocket watch. It was a lot better than the ones he had for sale. Sparrow's actually worked. "I was wondering if you might want to buy this from me?"

The vendor took the watch. "You got permission to sell this?"

Sparrow reckoned she did. In her opinion, everything in Dalton House was hers. "Yes, sir."

He rubbed his sunburned nose. "How much do you want for it?"

"Thirty dollars." If Sparrow was selling something for money, she wanted to get as much as she could.

"I'll give you ten."

"I've got to get at least twenty-five."

"I'll give you ten."

Sparrow pursed her lips. Ten dollars didn't help. "Twenty."

"Ten." The vendor crossed his arms, tucking the watch out of sight.

Sparrow held her hand out for the watch. She wasn't taking a bad deal.

Reluctantly, the vendor placed it in her palm. "You'll be back. Ten dollars is a good price."

"It's an antique."

The watch vendor scoffed. "Sell it to a collector, then."

Sparrow looked toward Elena's van. A man sat in a lawn chair behind the antiquities booth reading a newspaper. "I will."

"You'll be back," the vendor called as Sparrow walked toward Elena's van.

The man minding the antiquities booth didn't have the line that Elena did. He didn't have a line at all.

Sparrow walked up to his booth. The man was so engrossed in what he was reading that he didn't notice Sparrow. She cleared her throat.

He looked up. His dark hair was cut short and he wore geeky glasses that somehow gave off an air of trendy chic. His clothes were simple but looked purposely casual, and he had a tattoo on his forearm that Sparrow couldn't see well enough to read. He seemed surprised to have a customer. "Are you here to see me?"

"Yep. I mean, yes, sir."

The man smiled. "Well, that's nice. My niece has been stealing my thunder all morning."

Sparrow glanced over to Elena's tent. Old Miss Annabelle was having her fortune told. Miss Annabelle was the oldest living Beulah resident. She had to be ninety-one at least. Sparrow wondered what kind of fortune she hoped for.

"You're Elena's uncle."

"That's right. I'm Eli."

"Nice to meet you, Mr. Eli. I'm Sparrow."

Eli chuckled. "I do love your southern manners, but you can call me Eli."

"I'll try. You know there's a good article about Elena in the paper."

"I know. I read it." He held up the *Beulah Herald*. "What can I do for you?"

"Do you buy antiques as well as sell them?"

"I do. Selectively."

"I have an antique pocket watch for sale." Sparrow pulled out the watch and displayed it across her palm to make her offer more enticing.

"That's lovely. May I?"

Sparrow handed Eli the watch.

He looked over the outside carefully, and then clicked open the cover.

Sparrow rocked up to her tiptoes so she could see the watch better. "It's only brass, but it works."

He checked his watch. "Correct time too. Beautiful specimen." He handed it back to Sparrow.

"Don't you want to buy it?"

"No, you take that back home. I can't know for certain without closer examination, but I think that's gold. Not brass. If so, your watch might be worth a small fortune."

"This old thing?" The pocket watch had been neglected

for years. Anyone attached to it no longer lived at Dalton House. "No one wants it. How much will you give me?"

"It's too valuable. It wouldn't be right to take that from you. Wait until you're older. Then you can decide if you still want to sell it."

Sparrow didn't have time to wait. It had been days since her one card reading with Elena. The peace she had felt at knowing Mama was trying to contact her had drained away, leaving her anxious and desperate for reassurance. The only person she knew who could give her that was Elena. "I need money *now*. For a tarot card reading."

Eli sighed heavily. "That watch is worth a thousand tarot card readings. Well, that is, if tarot card readings were actually worth something."

Sparrow squinted up at Eli. "Don't you believe in Elena's powers?" She remembered what Elena said about her mother. She thought tarot cards were ridiculous. It must be hard for Elena to have members of her family be skeptical of something that meant so much to her.

"I believe in letting kids explore their interests. My niece is precocious and I would never dream of stifling her, but don't trade a valuable antique for something so . . . unreliable."

"Hey, girlie," the watch vendor hollered, interrupting them. "You win. I'll give you twenty dollars for the watch."

Eli scowled at him. "Look, don't sell it to him. He knows it's valuable. He's counting on you not knowing its worth."

"I really need that reading." Sparrow bit her bottom lip. She had to find a way to contact Mama. Each second that ticked by without seeing her felt like a nail added to her coffin. "Thanks, anyway." She started toward the watch vendor.

The watch vendor rubbed his hands together. "I knew you'd be back."

"Wait," Eli called.

Sparrow turned around.

"If you're that desperate, I think I have an idea. Why don't you let me research it for you, and I'll tell Elena to give you the tarot card reading today. If it isn't as valuable as I think, we'll come up with a fair price. If it is, then we can work something else out."

"Is that fair to Elena?"

"Letting that swindler take advantage of you isn't fair. Elena will understand."

"If you're sure you can square it with her." Sparrow didn't like the idea of taking a handout.

"She'll be okay with it." He went to Elena's tent and whispered in her ear. Elena leaned around her uncle to look at Sparrow. She rolled her eyes. Sparrow hoped Eli had good powers of persuasion. Elena didn't seem enthusiastic about letting Sparrow have a free reading.

When he came back, he nodded. "It's all set. You let me keep this for a few days, and I'll find out what I can about it. In the meantime, Elena will give you that tarot card reading."

"Wow, thanks!" Sparrow couldn't believe her luck. Eli was a kind man. Elena was lucky to have an uncle like him. She wished she had a kind Uncle Eli instead of a grouchy Auntie Geraldine.

"Don't tell anyone, though. I don't think I could work the same deal twice. My niece is quite the entrepreneur."

"My lips are sealed." Sparrow handed over the watch and got in line after Clara.

By the time Sparrow's turn came up, she was hot, tired, and thirstier than a cypress tree, but she felt the wait had been worthwhile. As the sun had climbed higher and higher in the sky and the day grew hotter, the crowd had cleared. No one else waited behind Sparrow, which she considered a good omen. She didn't need half of Beulah eavesdropping on her conversation with Elena.

She took her place in the chair across from Elena. "Did your uncle tell you about the trade?"

"He did."

"Are you mad?"

Elena shuffled her deck of cards with her practiced expertise. "He promised to buy me ice cream every day until we got home. Sounded like a bargain." Elena's mouth twitched like she was suppressing a giggle, and for the second time, Sparrow glimpsed the kid behind the fortune-teller.

Beside Elena, a bundle of what looked like dried leaves bound together smoldered in a bowl. A small column of smoke emanated from the bundle and reminded Sparrow of the swirling spirits that seemed to be so fond of Johnny when they were in the graveyard the other day. "What's that bundle?"

"Sage. I use it as my cleansing ritual between clients. Keeps the energy clean and shoos away unwanted spirits." She picked it up and waved it enthusiastically, filling the air with smoke.

Sparrow resisted the urge to cough.

When there was a thick fog of smoke, Elena put the smoldering sage back into the bowl.

Sparrow waved her hand in front of her face, trying to clear the air.

"Do you need to put that out? It doesn't seem safe to leave it burning like that." Sparrow's primary concern was for Mama. As a spirit, Mama didn't seem to be strong yet. If she were, Sparrow felt sure she would have shown up by now. Sparrow worried that the shooing smoke might make it even harder for Mama to give her a message.

Elena flicked her hand dismissively, and her bangles collided with a clang. "It should be fine." She cut her deck of cards. "Are you ready?"

Sparrow nodded.

Elena said her incantation. "Spirits near, spirits far, spirits old, spirits new, come now and guide this seeker's hand."

Sparrow watched again to see if spirits joined them, and this time, as the air around them started to clear of the sage smoke, the Boy began to materialize beside Elena. He emerged slowly, fading in like an object coming into focus.

Elena knocked three times on the deck and began to deal the cards. "I'm going to put five cards on the table and then I'll read them like a story."

The smoke was almost completely gone now except for the thin stream that drifted up from the smoldering bundle, and the Boy looked almost solid. Only he moved lethargically, as if held at bay by something. Sparrow had never seen the Boy impeded before. He typically behaved as if he belonged in the living world as much as she did. Sparrow wondered if Elena knew her sage worked.

The Boy watched curiously as Elena put down cards.

Elena's well-loved cards were tattered and faded, but each had an intricately drawn picture on it. The first card Elena set down was the Page, the same card Sparrow had picked the other day. The next card she laid down showed a picture of a lady dressed in Victorian clothing. Then she dealt a card with an illustration of a book with a lock. After that, she placed a card with a key on the table. The last card she set down had a drawing of a tree that looked a lot like one of the oaks that shaded Sparrow's yard.

Elena swept up the rest of the deck and wrapped it in a silk scarf.

As Elena started to speak, the Boy leaned over her shoulder to get a better look. Elena shuddered as if she'd gotten a cold chill, and though she looked over her shoulder as if someone stood behind her, she did not comment on her reaction and Sparrow kept silent. The Boy was her secret.

"You remember the Page from the other day?"

Sparrow nodded.

"He's shown up again, so I'd take that to mean there is a message coming your way. The woman here represents someone dearly loved or sometimes a powerful ally. With the two cards next to each other, I'd suggest to you that the person trying to send you the message is someone trustworthy. Next, we have a diary with a lock. This represents a hidden secret but can also mean regret. Are you following me so far?"

"I think so." Obviously, Mama wanted to give Sparrow a message, but she already knew that.

"Good. Next we have a key and a tree. The tree also represents a person you can trust. This person is offering help. But to get that help, you need to make a sacrifice. More simply put, you need to do something for that person to get them to help you. Make sense?"

"Maybe." Elena's explanations sounded really vague. The person represented by the tree card could be anyone.

"The key means a solution is near or it can sometimes mean the solution is impossible. When I look at the cards all together, I think there is a secret you must solve to get the help you require." Elena sat back triumphantly.

Sparrow tried not to be disappointed, but she needed specific information, and everything Elena said could be interpreted in a hundred different ways.

Sparrow pointed at the last card. It reminded her of the view from her front porch on a sunny day. "It's a *tree*. How in the world do I figure out who it represents?"

"Typically, these things become clear in time," Elena said airily.

Sparrow bit her lip in frustration. She didn't want it to become clear in time. She wanted to know now.

The Boy slowly dissolved and Sparrow wondered if the sage smoke was too much for him after all, or if he had grown bored, as he sometimes did.

Sparrow pulled the tree card toward her, and the longer she looked at it, the more it reminded her of the view from her front porch. Only now it didn't look like a sunny day. It looked like a stormy one, with dark rolling clouds and even a flash of lightning in the far corner. It seemed so real. It almost looked as if the clouds were moving.

As Sparrow looked on, she realized she wasn't looking at an artist's trick. The clouds didn't just look like they were moving; they *were* moving. "Are they supposed to do that?"

Elena looked at the card. Her eyes grew wide and she pushed away from the table.

Sparrow felt a soft breeze tease her hair. Tendrils blew across her cheeks.

The tent billowed slightly and then deflated.

Sparrow looked up. The roof rippled like water and then stilled.

For the briefest moment, the world seemed to pause, as if time itself stopped moving. Then it sped up again.

The tent flew out and flapped about as gusts of wind tried to tear it from the ground.

Elena's cards blew off the table and Elena hopped up to chase after them.

Sparrow ran after Elena to help her gather the cards before the wind carried them all the way to town.

"Grab that card!" Elena tried to catch a card that tumbled out of reach. The card swirled about in an uncanny pattern that defied nature.

Suddenly, the day turned dark and the sky churned with black clouds.

A thunderstorm rolled toward Beulah.

When Sparrow had finally chased down the last card, she turned back to Elena. Elena stood under her flapping tent, staring at the little table.

Sparrow walked to Elena's side.

Two cards rested in the center of the table, untouched by the gusting wind—a coffin partially covered in a shroud and the picture of the tree.

CHAPTER TWELVE

"Elena," Sparrow said gently. "I think—"

Eli interrupted Sparrow. "Girls, you need to wrap it up. It looks like a bad storm is on its way. Elena, we need to get this stuff under cover."

Sparrow turned to Elena. Her arms were crossed over her chest and she glowered at Sparrow. "But . . ."

"I really think you need to get going. You don't want to get caught in that." Eli pointed at the sky.

Sparrow looked up. The Everglades were a capricious land, and the weather changed on a dime. Even though the sky awoke bright blue and singing that morning, it now rolled with thunderclouds black as night. The coming storm was a monster, and she needed to get home before the heavens opened up.

Sparrow didn't have time for explanations or questions now. She took off running.

By the time she reached the marsh, the wind no longer gusted in occasional puffs but whipped steadily. The reed

107

grass bent under its force, tips touching roots, and Sparrow knew she had mere moments before the rain came down.

It wasn't that she minded getting wet. It was the lightning that scared her.

Lightning struck people down in the Everglades.

Bright flashes lit the sky, and she counted Mississippis between bursts. Though miles away yet, lightning traveled fast. She needed to be faster. Sparrow picked up the pace and raced for home.

She managed to dart under the cover of the front porch as the rain started to pour. She let the screen door shut with a loud slap and plopped down on the swing, trying to catch her breath. From the safety of the porch, she watched round raindrops pound the land.

Like the weather of the Everglades, Sparrow was learning that grief wasn't a steady thing. It changed moment to moment, and the sadness she'd been able to set aside in the excitement of making plans and talking to Elena came back as furious as the storm.

Sparrow felt as bleak as the rain.

She looked up at the dark clouds and whispered a pleading prayer to beg for what she wanted more than anything else in the world—Mama back.

She closed her eyes and waited.

Like a miracle, she felt a soft, spectral hand slide into hers. For a moment, she let herself believe her wish had come true, and then she turned.

The Boy sat beside her and held her hand. He stared at her with dark eyes so lonely she felt she might drown in the depths of their sadness. She'd never noticed before how unhappy he seemed, but now that she had, she wondered how she'd ever missed it.

Abashed, she looked down.

Lying in the sliver of space between them like a gift was the tree card.

Sparrow picked it up. The threadbare paper felt as supple as well-worn cotton and as precious as a promise. Her heart fluttered.

The Boy was the tree. He was offering to help her find Mama.

Sparrow met the Boy's eyes. Looking into them was like gazing at her own lonely soul. She imagined him wandering Dalton House, adrift and abandoned. She recalled the rest of Elena's prediction—he needed her help in return.

Sparrow nodded to let the Boy know she understood.

He gave her a slow, sad smile, and Sparrow got the sense that he'd waited her entire life for her to recognize his need. She knew what it felt like to wait for something that never came. A rush of compassion engulfed her. She felt his pain as if it were her own, and her heart cracked.

A tear rolled down her cheek.

The Boy wiped the falling tear with his ghostly hand.

Sparrow felt it drop on hers.

Sparrow and the Boy stayed linked together, watching each other, watching the rain, and holding hands until they heard the sound of Auntie Geraldine's tires on the gravel drive.

"Sparrow?" Auntie Geraldine pushed open the screen door, her red dress a shock of color amid the dreary backdrop of the day.

The Boy faded away.

Sparrow quickly wiped her face. The Boy's promise to find Mama filled her with a bittersweet peace. Knowing he planned to help bring Mama back soothed the ache in her soul, but it also made her feel sad that the Boy had waited so long for the same feeling.

If Auntie Geraldine noticed Sparrow's tears, she chose not to comment. Instead, she shook her umbrella, sprinkling water everywhere.

"It's bad luck to have an open umbrella in the house," Sparrow said, repeating the superstition Mama frequently quoted when chiding Sparrow for poor manners more than tempting fate. Everyone knew it was rude to drip rainwater on the floor.

Auntie Geraldine yanked her umbrella shut. "This is not *in* the house. This is *on* the front porch."

Sparrow spent so much time on the porch sitting on her swing that it felt like the living room to her. She contemplated explaining this very sensible distinction to Auntie Geraldine, but she was interrupted before she got the chance.

"There are groceries in the car. Go get them."

Sparrow wanted to remind Auntie Geraldine that she had not said please but decided Auntie Geraldine was too old to learn manners anyway, so it wasn't worth the bother. Besides, Sparrow didn't feel the need to train Auntie Geraldine. The Boy had promised to help her find Mama, and nothing Auntie Geraldine did could upset her now.

Sparrow dashed out to the Buick to grab the groceries. There were three grocery bags in the trunk, all filled with blue-and-white boxes of salt. Sparrow couldn't think of one reason to need all that salt. Auntie Geraldine must finally be losing her mind. Sparrow scooped up two of the bags, and when she saw what was underneath, her heart plummeted all the way to her stomach. A FOR SALE sign hid on the bottom of the trunk like an invader.

Sparrow stared at the sign in horror as raindrops fell, soaking her to the bone. In that moment, she realized she'd never truly believed Auntie Geraldine would sell the house and make her move away. A furious, raging anger filled Sparrow from her head to her toes. Auntie Geraldine hated Sparrow. She had to. Why else would she remove Sparrow from the house she loved, the house where all her memories were, the house the Boy lived in, the place most likely for Mama to come to when she returned? She was only doing it out of meanness, spite, and hate.

Sparrow refused to let her get away with it.

Sparrow grabbed the bags and pounded up the porch steps. She walked into the kitchen and dropped the bags at Auntie Geraldine's feet. They thudded to the ground. The boxes of salt tumbled out and broke apart, spewing grainy white salt all over the kitchen floor.

"What in the name of creation is wrong with you?"

"The house. You're going to sell it."

"That's not been a secret. You've known that the entire time. I can't live in this horrible old place."

"*You're* horrible."

Auntie Geraldine stalked over to Sparrow and grabbed her by the arm. "You listen here. You are insufferable and rude. I should sell you with the house." The rain took on a new tenor, coming down so hard the noise from the tin roof sounded like an army on the march. Auntie Geraldine looked up at the roof as if she might be able to see the rain. "Did you shut the trunk?" She had to yell to be heard over the clatter.

"I did not," Sparrow yelled back.

Auntie Geraldine dropped Sparrow's arm and rushed toward the door.

Sparrow hated that car. It was the only thing Auntie Geraldine loved. "I hope it drowns."

Auntie Geraldine paused midstride and spun back to Sparrow. Her face was pure fury, and her red dress made her look like an executioner. "Don't you EVER say *drowned* in this house. Not this close to the marsh. That land out there that you think is so wonderful. It is hard and cruel. It turns on a dime. Tease it and you might find out what it's capable of."

Auntie Geraldine's speech stunned Sparrow. She'd never known her to be superstitious. She was practical and efficient.

Auntie Geraldine seemed to have surprised herself with her lecture, but she recovered quickly. "I'm glad to see that I've finally made you lose your sass. Get this kitchen cleaned up and then go to your room. I don't want you in my sight the rest of the night. And if you EVER talk to me like that again, I will find something you love and shred it to

113

pieces." Auntie Geraldine stormed out of the kitchen, her black pumps hitting the hardwood with so much force indentions followed in her wake.

Sparrow felt the hot sting of tears. Auntie Geraldine had done that already. Sparrow felt like her life was being torn apart little by little each day.

She grabbed the broom and started to sweep, putting all her anger into the act. When she had a huge, round mound of salt, she opened up the back door and shoved it out into the rain.

Sparrow had to stop Auntie Geraldine from selling the house and she needed someone to help her. Fortunately, she had the perfect person in mind—Mason Casto.

CHAPTER THIRTEEN

It rained for four days, and almost as if the marsh had set out to prove Auntie Geraldine's point, its waters rose higher and higher with each drop. The marsh covered the mudflats and the sandbar. By the third day, it crested the banks and its watery tendrils lapped at the lawn and soaked the ground up to the porch steps.

Those were lonely days for Sparrow.

As much as she tried to be hopeful about the Boy's promise to help find Mama, a flood of grief and setbacks arrived with the rain.

Auntie Geraldine refused to speak to Sparrow, and while Sparrow disliked much of what Auntie Geraldine had to say when she did talk, the silence hit her hard. Being trapped in Dalton House for four days with a vengeful Auntie Geraldine made Sparrow miss Mama in a whole new way. Sparrow was hurting, and she needed the kindness of comfort. She yearned to travel back in time to when she was a little kid and Mama fixed even the biggest problems with a hug and a kiss.

To compound her sorrow, the Boy had mysteriously disappeared, and his absence made Sparrow feel hollow.

She had not seen him since the afternoon on the porch when he held her hand and promised to help her find Mama. Up until that moment, Sparrow had seen him every day of her life. He was her closest companion, her link to Mama, and the life raft that kept her afloat when the swell of grief threatened to overflow. To be parted from him felt like drowning.

The Boy's inexplicable disappearance distressed Sparrow so much that when the fifth day dawned with a bright, gleaming sun and white clouds that drifted across the blue sky like sailing ships, she knew she needed to do something to unravel the mystery of his unnerving departure.

She planned to tell Elena about the Boy. Elena knew about sage smoke and tarot cards and mystical truths—if there was anyone who could help her figure out where the Boy had gone, it was Elena, and Sparrow had run out of time to be coy. With the Boy missing, the house up for sale, and Mama nowhere to be seen, Sparrow had to take desperate measures.

After Sparrow told Elena about the Boy, she was going to talk to Mason Casto. She needed someone to save the house from Auntie Geraldine, and if the rumors were true, and Mason *had* made a fortune in the oil business and *was* her daddy, he might want to buy Dalton House for her. She'd been daydreaming about it so frequently since the thought first popped into her head that the prospect felt almost as real as a memory.

Sparrow walked into the kitchen and paused. Theirs was a country kitchen with walls the color of buttermilk and sheer white curtains that billowed when the breeze blew just right. The radio that sat on the kitchen counter played a country hymn, and the music called up Mama in a way that made Sparrow ache. Mama always listened to old country hymns on the radio and lately, Sparrow often heard it playing softly. Auntie Geraldine turned it on in the mornings and let it play all day and into the night. At first, Sparrow thought Auntie Geraldine did it to hurt her. Then, after watching Auntie Geraldine closely during those days of silence, Sparrow wondered if she turned it on for other reasons.

Auntie Geraldine wasn't in the kitchen. Instead, a piece of yellow legal paper sat in the middle of the table. Sparrow walked across the room to retrieve the note and heard the crunch of salt under her feet. Despite multiple sweeping episodes, the salt lingered with a puzzling tenacity. Sparrow felt sure that living in a sea of perpetual salt annoyed Auntie Geraldine, and this thought gave Sparrow a twinge of satisfaction every time she heard it crunch under her feet.

Sparrow picked up the note. Auntie Geraldine had scrawled, *Gone to Wesley Monroe's. Back soon. You are still forbidden to go to town!*

Sparrow wrote back, *Not in town! Outside. Back soon.*

She felt proud of her cryptic message. Outside covered a lot of territory. Hopefully, Auntie Geraldine would assume Sparrow wandered the property and wouldn't go looking for her.

Sparrow walked down the driveway to the main road instead of taking the more hidden route beside the marsh. It was riskier to go that way, but she didn't have a choice. The marsh water was still high from all the rain, and Auntie Geraldine's warnings made Sparrow uneasy. She had always believed the marsh to be friendly. Now Auntie Geraldine's words echoed in her head, planting doubts. Auntie Geraldine ruined everything.

When Sparrow got to the end of the driveway, she saw the FOR SALE sign. She yanked it up and tossed it down. Even though the day was as still as church, she shoved it with her toe to make it look askew, as if the wind had knocked it over. Auntie Geraldine would probably figure Sparrow had done it, but she didn't care. She would do anything to keep the house from being sold. Dalton House was theirs. It belonged to Mama and Sparrow, and she refused to let it go without a fight.

Sparrow arrived at the flea market to find a very different scene than before the rain. Even though the sun shone, everything was still wet from the storm. The vendors manned their booths, but they appeared to be drying out their merchandise rather than selling it.

Sparrow made her way to Elena's van and discovered the situation there to be the same as the rest of the flea market. The antiquities booth had nothing on display, and Elena's tent sat deserted.

Sparrow knocked on the side of the van.

The sliding door pulled back to reveal Elena. Though it took Sparrow a moment to recognize the fortune-teller. She didn't look like herself. She wore shorts and a T-shirt instead of a fashionable sundress. Her chestnut hair was plaited in twin braids rather than down, and she wore no jewelry.

The most shocking shift was in her demeanor. Elena seemed younger, as if the fortune-teller had stepped aside and let the girl Sparrow kept glimpsing take over.

"What are *you* doing here?" Elena asked.

Sparrow had come to ask for Elena's help, but Elena looked like she needed a friend. "Are you okay?"

"Like you care." Elena crossed her arms. Not in a challenging way like Maeve, but defensively, protecting herself.

"I do." Sparrow did care. She liked Elena. "Do you think we can talk?"

Elena didn't answer. She simply moved aside and went to the back of the van.

Sparrow climbed in after her. Once inside, the van looked more like a mini-house than a vehicle. The roof popped up to make a loft bed, and instead of traditional seats, there was a table with benches. The word *groovy* came to mind even though Sparrow never said it.

Elena sat at the table with a deck of cards. Only these were not tarot cards, just a regular deck. It looked like Elena was playing a game of solitaire. Elena focused on her game, ignoring Sparrow.

"Are you mad at me?" Sparrow didn't know what she had done. What had happened with the Boy during the reading was strange, but she didn't expect Elena to be upset about that. Elena was an expert on tarot cards and fortunes. Surely, she had experience with spirits too.

Elena glared at her. "I'm sure you had a good laugh at the weird girl from up north."

"What are you talking about?"

Elena's jaw clenched. "Your practical joke the other day when you made that strange stuff happen before the storm. It was very funny. Did you and your friends have a good laugh?"

"I would never do something like that." Sparrow had

been made fun of too often to purposely make someone else feel bad. "I'm the person people make fun of."

"Yeah, right. Look at you. You're confident and sure of yourself, and Eli says you're super smart. He said you haggled with that watch vendor like a pro. Who would make fun of you?"

"Practically every kid in town." It surprised Sparrow to hear Elena describe her with the same words she'd use to describe Elena. It also felt good. Beulah folks didn't like Sparrow much, but here were these outsiders seeing her with new eyes. It made Sparrow wonder if she saw herself clearly.

"Why did you do it, then? Make all that weird stuff happen with the cards?"

"I didn't. I swear. That's why I wanted to come talk to you . . ." Sparrow paused. She wondered if she was truly ready to share the secret of the Boy. Even as a little kid, she never told anyone about him, but now he was gone, Mama had not been seen, and Auntie Geraldine was selling the house. Sparrow needed help, and Elena knew about these things, but it was more than that. Elena was the first person Sparrow had met who felt like a kindred spirit. Elena loved her tarot cards the way Sparrow loved her porch swing. Elena felt passionate about her family legacy, the same way

Sparrow felt passionate about Dalton House. Elena believed in mystics and Sparrow saw spirits. If Sparrow was going to risk opening up to someone, Elena was a good choice.

"You were saying?" Elena played another card. This time she put a red queen over a black king.

"The Boy did that thing with your cards. Only now he's missing, and I thought you might know why."

"*The Boy?* Right. You can let it go already. You got me. Ha ha."

Sparrow had finally gotten brave enough to talk about the Boy, and she'd messed it up. Elena thought Sparrow was teasing her. "I'm not joking."

Elena's expression hardened. "Yes, you are. You're just like the kids at school, making fun of me because I'm interested in fortune-telling. You think I'm weird, but I'm not. It was my grandmother's legacy to me and if I don't keep it alive, no one else will. My mom thinks it is ridiculous. My dad agrees with her. Even Eli doesn't care about it, and he's interested in all kinds of historical things. At least with Eli, he understands why it matters to me."

Sparrow understood why fortune-telling mattered to Elena. She knew what it was like to try to hold on to something that was slipping away. Sparrow pulled Elena's tarot card from her back pocket and sat next to her. "I promise I'm not making fun of you." She slid the tree card across the table to Elena as a peace offering. "I'm sorry if you've been missing this. I know your cards are special."

Elena pulled the card toward her. "How did you get this?"

"I told you. The Boy."

Elena looked up from the tree card and scrutinized Sparrow. "*The Boy?*"

"He's a ghost. He's a bit of a prankster. He did that thing with your cards, but he wasn't trying to scare you or be mean. He was trying to communicate with me. He wants me to help him."

Elena tossed a braid over her shoulder. "So you're *psychic?*"

"No, I'm not psychic, but I do see spirits. Mostly, the Boy. I don't know who he is or why I see him." Sparrow shrugged. "I just always have."

"You know the definition of a psychic is a person who sees ghosts." Elena still looked skeptical, but her tone had shifted from angry to sarcastic. Sparrow was encouraged. Elena was warming up.

"Do you see them?" Sparrow asked.

Elena shut down again and glared at Sparrow. "No."

Sparrow forged ahead. "Look, I don't know anyone like you. You know so much about all this stuff, and I really need some help. The Boy went missing, and I don't know why. Will you help me figure it out?"

Elena took a deep breath as if steeling herself for the conversation ahead. "When did this happen?"

"The last time I saw him was on my front porch the day I saw you. He was at the reading, but the sage made him kind of strange."

"When you say he was at the reading, what do you mean?"

"He was standing behind you, looking over your shoulder. I think you might have felt him. You shivered and looked behind you."

Elena perked up, suddenly very interested. "Seriously? I remember feeling suddenly cold, like someone had touched me with icy hands. Are you telling me that was your ghost?"

Sparrow nodded. "Do you think the sage could have hurt him? Made him weak somehow?"

Elena reached for the tree card and started to play with it. "I don't know. It's possible, I suppose, but doubtful. Are you burning sage at your house or have you ever burned sage there?"

"No." Sparrow had never even seen sage until her reading with Elena.

"I don't think it is the sage. Sage is one of many cleansing tools. But you would have had to burn it at your house for it to affect him there. Besides, you said he showed up at the reading anyway. Despite the sage?"

"That's right." Sparrow knew talking to Elena was a good idea. They were already starting to sort out a few things, and doing something, even if it was only talking through the problem, made Sparrow feel more hopeful and less alone.

"And you usually see him there, no problem?"

"That's right."

Elena tapped her fingers on the tree card. "It must take an awful lot of energy to appear like that. Maybe now that he's asked you for help, he's gone away until you can figure out what he needs?"

"*Maybe.*" Sparrow sighed heavily. She was so frustrated. Everything hinged on figuring out what the Boy wanted, but she didn't even know where to start looking for clues. With him gone, she might never find out what he needed. "But I have no idea what he needs."

"Peace. That's what all ghosts need," Elena said with complete confidence.

But the Boy had peace. Living at Dalton House was heaven. The porch swing, the marsh. It was the perfect place to spend eternity. *The perfect place for Sparrow.* She recalled the way the Boy's eyes looked when they held hands on the porch. A soul at peace could never have eyes that sorrowful. "How do you give them peace?"

"You find out what they need to move on. Spirits are supposed to pass over. When they don't, something is wrong.

They stay behind because they have unfinished business. Figure out what their unfinished business is, help them finish it, and voilà . . . they cross over."

Sparrow didn't like the turn the conversation had taken. Her goal was to bring spirits back, not help them cross over. But she did agree that the Boy must have something he wanted Sparrow to do for him. She learned that at the reading. Elena had said the person the tree card represented would help Sparrow with what she needed, but she needed to provide help in return. The Boy was the tree.

"Do you know anything about who he was?"

"No, but he's got to be a Dalton since he lives at my house."

"You'll have to find out who he was, so you can sort out what is holding him here. It's the only way to set him free. Once you do, he'll stop haunting you."

The van windows were opened to allow for a breeze, but it was a windless day, so it didn't offer any relief from the weather. It did, however, let in the scent of Beulah. Beulah smelled like salt water, reed grass, and heat all mixed together, and reminded Sparrow of everything she loved—Dalton House, Mama, the Boy. She didn't want him to stop haunting her.

Before she could tell Elena she didn't want to set him free, she wanted to bring him home, she heard a rustle under the window and someone whisper-yell, "No way! Sparrow is haunted."

Sparrow's stomach flip-flopped. Someone was spying on them. She wondered how much they'd heard. She didn't need all of Beulah knowing about the Boy.

Sparrow and Elena rushed to the window and looked out.

Hiding in the bushes were Maeve and Johnny. Maeve smacked Johnny on the head and shushed him.

"Friends?" Elena pointed at them.

"Yes." Sparrow hoped it was still true now that they knew about her ghost.

CHAPTER FOURTEEN

Sparrow, Maeve, and Johnny walked along the road away from town.

Johnny walked beside Maeve, loyal as ever, his hands in his pockets and his head down. He stared at his bare feet like they were the most interesting things in the world. He hadn't said much since the flea market, and Sparrow worried he didn't like her now that he knew about the Boy, or worse, was afraid of her. Sparrow was used to the Boy's ways and could see him, so he didn't scare her. It consoled her to know that the soul lived on after death. It meant Mama's soul lived. Johnny might not feel the same way, though.

Maeve, on the other hand, wasn't upset at all. In fact, she was elated. She practically danced beside Sparrow as they walked. She'd been asking her questions nonstop. "So, let me get this straight. Your ghost showed up during your fortune to communicate with you?"

"Yes," Sparrow said.

"And the fortune-teller doesn't know what he was

trying to tell you even though she saw two tarot cards stuck to a table during a windstorm?" Maeve asked.

"She thinks I need to find out who he was, so I can figure out what his unfinished business is and help him finish it," Sparrow said.

"Only now you've lost your ghost, so you can't prove his existence to us by making him do something?"

Sparrow didn't like Maeve's way of putting it, but she supposed she summed it up perfectly. "I can't *make* him do stuff anyway. He does what he wants."

"We just have to take your word for it that you're haunted? Not that we don't believe you. But it sure would be cool to see him do something. Right, Johnny?" Maeve elbowed her brother.

Sparrow wondered if Maeve would really like to see the Boy pulling one of his pranks, moving things around that should stay still. It might scare her.

Johnny made a noncommittal sound, and Sparrow felt a nervous twinge. Maybe he was deciding he didn't want to be her friend anymore.

"And you can see him?" Maeve asked for the thousandth time. "Plain as day? So, if he were around you'd know."

"Yes." To talk about the Boy after years of silence felt strange, like walking on dry land after poling through the marsh on a raft. While there was relief in finally being able to share her secret with other people, it threw her off balance.

"Oh, boy! Oh, boy!" Maeve threw her arm around Sparrow's shoulder and pulled her close. "I knew being related to a Dalton was going to be great, but you're the best cousin ever!" She squeezed Sparrow, hugging her against her side, and Sparrow savored the comfort of being linked with another.

Johnny looked at the two girls. He seemed completely befuddled at his sister's affectionate treatment of Sparrow.

Sparrow got that twinge of doubt again. "You still want to be related to me?"

Maeve gaped at her. "Don't be stupid. We want to be related to you now more than ever. I mean, before you were just strange. Now you're interesting."

Sparrow wanted to laugh, but she was too worried about Johnny. Maeve might speak over her brother constantly, but that didn't mean she spoke for him. Johnny might feel differently.

"What about you, Johnny?" Sparrow asked softly.

"I don't want to be related to you because you can see ghosts."

"Oh."

Johnny's brow furrowed and he stuffed his hands deeper into his pockets. "What I mean is I don't want to be related to you because you can see ghosts or because you're a Dalton, I want to be related to you because we're family. Family just is. And I want you to have a daddy, especially now that your mama isn't around. And because my uncle Mason is a great guy and he's lonely. He has all of us Castos, but it isn't the same as having a kid of his own."

Johnny's words wrapped around Sparrow like one of Mama's hugs. She felt wanted for the first time since Mama died. Sparrow blinked back tears. The Castos were full of surprises.

Maeve smiled proudly at her brother. "Besides, the two of them are a good match. He's a little strange too."

Johnny smirked and Sparrow laughed. A little weird did sound like a good match. Sparrow began to ask Maeve and Johnny the best way to talk to Mason about being her dad, but Maeve started pelting her with questions again.

"Wait." Maeve looked around her. "You're *sure* he's not following us now, right?"

"I'm sure."

"Are other ghosts following us? Do you see them all the time?"

Sparrow thought about the swirling spirits and her inability to see Mama even though she wanted to more than anything in the world. She hadn't told Maeve, Johnny, or Elena about that part. If she did, Elena might wonder if she was making fun of her again and Maeve might try to hold a séance right there on the side of the road. Johnny might understand, but her grasp on the differences and the connections felt too nebulous, like trying to hold on to water, so she kept that piece to herself for the moment.

"I don't think it works that way."

"So let me get this straight. When you got home after having your fortune told, you and this Boy had a moment, and now Elena thinks you have to figure out who he was and what he wants to get him to come back?"

Maeve had summed up the situation pretty well. The Boy held the key to bringing Mama back, but now she'd lost him too. Without him, there was no hope at all.

"Yes, but I'm not sure where to start now. I thought Elena might know a . . . spell or something to bring him back."

"I'm not sure about spells to bring ghosts back, but if I was looking for one, I'd go to the graveyard," Johnny said wisely.

Maeve slapped her brother on the shoulder. "That makes perfect sense!"

It did. Except Sparrow hadn't been back there since the day Andrew had chased them, and the thought of Mama's grave made her heart heavy.

"Yeah, that makes sense."

"Let's go, then." Maeve started off and then turned back when she realized Sparrow and Johnny were not moving. "Um . . . what are we waiting for?"

"Sparrow might not want to go right this second, Maeve," Johnny said.

"What? Why not?"

Johnny shrugged.

"Maeve's right. We should go now," Sparrow said.

"Darn right, I'm right! Let's go!" Maeve walked back to Sparrow and Johnny and linked her arms in their arms. "This is turning out to be the best summer ever!"

Johnny sighed, clearly exasperated with his sister's insensitivity.

"*What?*" Maeve looked from one to the other. "Look, I know Sparrow lost her mama and that is the worst thing ever, but it doesn't mean she has to be sad all the time. I think it's okay for her to look on the bright side every once in a while."

Again, Maeve had phrased things differently than Sparrow would have, but she thought she'd said it well just the same anyway.

Maeve gently pulled them forward, and the three of them were on their way to the graveyard.

CHAPTER FIFTEEN

It was Maeve's idea to pick the flowers.

As they walked, they gathered the wildflowers that grew along the road. By the time they reached the grave-yard, they had an impressive collection of blazing stars, a scraggly flower with more green stems than lavender buds. They scrunched it together to make something resembling a bouquet. It looked a little weedy, but all of them were proud of their offering, and Sparrow thought Mama would like it. She had been gifted at seeing beauty where others did not.

Sparrow set the scraggly bundle at the base of Mama's headstone. When she let go, the flowers separated, making them look more like weeds than a bouquet.

Maeve bent down and scrunched them up, intertwining the brittle stems, so they stuck together. "That's better."

Sparrow smiled. It was. When Maeve stepped away, they only fell apart a little bit, and Sparrow thought Mama would like their messy perfection.

"Okay, so let's look for this ghost." Maeve put her hands on her hips and scanned the tiny graveyard. "He's not here with us, right?"

Maeve had been asking Sparrow this every five minutes for the entire walk. "No, he's not. I told you he's gone," Sparrow said, repeating herself for the thousandth time. Though there were spirits in the graveyard, the swirly, wispy kind. They swarmed around Johnny like bees about a honeycomb. They were so thick that Sparrow marveled at his apparent inability to sense them. He seemed completely oblivious to their presence.

"We need to look for angels or lambs or small headstones. That's what they always put for children," Johnny said.

"How do you know that?" Maeve asked.

"I read," Johnny answered.

"He does," Maeve told Sparrow. "All the time. It's really annoying."

Sparrow wished she could say the idea of Johnny Casto reading a book didn't shock her, but it did. He didn't have a reputation as a good student. Most considered him, and all other Castos, barely literate, but it seemed that assumption was way off base.

"All right, then; let's look for small headstones, lambs, or angels," Sparrow said.

"How old would you say he is? I mean was . . . when he

died? Or how old does he look to you?" Johnny asked, clearly unsure of the right way to speak about a ghost. Sparrow wasn't sure there was a right way.

"Ten or eleven, I think, and his clothes are formal-looking. Like they could be from a long time ago or church clothes."

Maeve gaped at Sparrow. "You see him that clearly?"

"Yes." She had already told Maeve this.

"And you're not scared? Ever?" Maeve asked.

"No, not really. I mean, he's just a kid like us. Only he's a spirit." Sparrow had already told Maeve this too. She was starting to feel like a roadside attraction.

Maeve let out a low whistle.

"Okay, so we're looking for a child ten or eleven, possibly buried a long time ago. Right?" Johnny asked.

Sparrow nodded.

"It will go quicker if we spread out. I'll look over there; Maeve, you look in that direction, and Sparrow, why don't you take over by the gate?" Johnny said, doling out assignments. It wasn't a large graveyard, but there were still a lot of headstones packed into the small space.

"I'll look over there, and you look in that direction," Maeve said, switching up the tasks.

Johnny sighed. "Fine, but don't do a Maeve look."

"What's that supposed to mean?"

Johnny stared at his sister knowingly.

Maeve rolled her eyes. "Fine, Mr. Know-it-all."

The three went in their appointed directions.

Sparrow went by the gate and started looking at head-stones. She recognized most of the last names etched into the stones. Beulah families were loyal ones, and most stayed in town their entire life. In fact, Mason Casto was the only person she'd ever known who'd left it, and now even he'd found his way back.

All the headstones listed the date of the person's death along with their birthdate. Sparrow guesstimated the age of the older ones by looking at the span of numbers, but when they'd died in midlife like Mama, it made the math harder. The baby headstones were the saddest. Some were only a few days old when they died.

Sparrow was brushing away debris from a child's head-stone when she heard the gate creak. She looked up. Eli was entering the graveyard. He was dressed nicely in clothes Sparrow typically saw men wear only on Sunday.

Sparrow stood up.

She seemed to startle him, and he paused. "Sorry, Sparrow. I didn't mean to disturb you."

"It's okay," Sparrow said. "You didn't."

He scanned the graveyard, and his eyes fell on Maeve and Johnny, who hadn't noticed the newcomer. They were both engrossed in reading headstones. "School project?"

"Kind of," Sparrow said. "Trying to find out information about someone who might have lived a long time ago."

"That's my specialty. I'm a history professor." He pushed his shirtsleeves up his arms, and the tattoo peeked out briefly. It was a phrase, but Sparrow couldn't read it before the sleeves fell back down and the tattoo disappeared.

"But you're an antique dealer."

"Only sometimes. My real job is a professor."

"Huh." He didn't look much like a history professor. The word *professor* made Sparrow think of a white-haired man with a pipe. He looked on the younger side and had a tattoo. Not very professory, in Sparrow's opinion.

He smiled. "I know. No gray hair or pipe."

"How did you know I was thinking that?"

"Hunch."

"Is that what you're here to do? Read headstones?"

He shrugged. "Investigating a few things. Speaking of research, do you mind if I keep your watch for a few more days?"

"Sparrow! Sparrow! Sparrow! I think I found something," Maeve called from across the graveyard.

"Nope—I mean, no, sir."

Eli chuckled. "Love those manners. I wonder if I can teach Elena to call me sir."

"Sparrow!" Maeve called again.

"Just a sec, I think she'll keep hollering if I don't go over there."

"Of course."

Sparrow dashed over to Maeve. "Did you find something?"

"Maybe." Maeve pointed to a simple grave marker rubbed raw by time. Covered in moss and damp from Beulah's constant humidity, the tombstone looked swamp touched.

Sparrow knelt down next to Maeve. She ran her hand over the cold stone, sweeping aside remnants of gray moss and dried grass. As soon as she touched the stone, a group of swirling spirits descended, encircling the grave marker. The spirits made no noise. They were as voiceless as the Boy, but Sparrow got the distinct impression they wailed as if they lamented this death. The power of their grief overwhelmed Sparrow. It felt like the pull of an undertow, and she yanked her hand away to keep from getting sucked under.

"Everything okay?" Maeve asked.

"Yes, sorry."

Maeve's expression told Sparrow she didn't believe her, but in a very un-Maeve-like way, she let it go. "The dates place him at the right age, but the name has been worn away, and there's no inscription. Poor kid. He doesn't even have an angel or a lamb to keep him company."

Sparrow cradled her hands to keep herself from reaching out again. The swirling spirits blanketed the tomb as if they protected it. "It feels sad here."

Maeve reached her hand to the stone and gingerly stroked it in another very un-Maeve-like way. The spirits disassembled and parted, allowing her passage through their veil. They approved of her homage. "Johnny! Come over here!"

Johnny jogged up beside the girls. "What did you find?"

"Sparrow's ghost."

CHAPTER SIXTEEN

By the time they'd finished looking at the headstone, Eli had gone. This turn of events disappointed Sparrow. She liked Eli and wanted to talk to him some more. Talking to people who came from different parts of the country reminded her that life was made up of more than Castos, Daltons, and Monroes, and that made her world feel bigger.

Maeve nudged Sparrow in the ribs to get her attention. "He's got to be the one, right?"

Sparrow didn't know. She'd had a strong reaction to the grave, but the Boy hadn't shown himself. She expected to see him or at least see a sign from him to let her know she was on the right track, but he remained missing.

"It makes sense. If that is his grave, something sad happened to him. It's almost like he was put in that corner to be forgotten."

Maeve shuddered. "I'd hate to be put in the ground without even a lamb to keep me company and no inscription to say anything nice about me!"

"It's heartbreaking." Sparrow remembered the stone Auntie Geraldine put at Mama's grave. It was a marker of remembrance, not of forgetting. She'd done right by Mama and Sparrow in that small act. A rush of gratitude for Auntie Geraldine flowed through Sparrow. Then she recalled the FOR SALE sign and Auntie Geraldine's plan to take her away, and the anger surged back. Getting one part right didn't absolve Auntie Geraldine of the rest.

Johnny nodded his agreement. Sparrow was learning that Johnny wasn't much of a talker. He usually waited until he had something to say before speaking, said it, and then clammed up again. It was probably why the spirits liked him so much.

Maeve, on the other hand, chatted endlessly.

Sparrow liked both approaches and both Castos immensely. She'd never had a circle of friends before. At school, everyone clumped in groups, except Sparrow. She spent most of her time alone. The other kids overlooked her as if she were as much of a ghost as the Boy. She liked the comfort of her newfound group. It made everything easier.

Sparrow recalled her earlier conversation with Elena. She had mentioned that knowing who the Boy had been in life would help Sparrow figure out what was preventing him from finding peace. That logic made sense to Sparrow. Coming to the graveyard had been a good beginning, but with an unmarked gravestone as their only clue, it felt like starting back at square one. Tomorrow she'd find Elena and tell her what they'd discovered. Sparrow hoped Elena would have advice about what to do next.

The three kids started along the main road back to town. The day had turned oppressive, the heat so stifling it felt like walking through the swamp rather than near it.

Maeve pushed her red hair back from her face. "I'm practically . . . well, I was going to say dying, but it seems tacky. Anyway, I'm parched. Anyone got money?"

"Nope," Johnny said.

"Nope," Sparrow said.

"Figures. You know, if we stop by the 76 station and look pathetic enough, Uncle Mason might buy us Cokes from the gas station vending machine," Maeve said.

"Great idea. He's been feeling sentimental about family since he got back to town," Johnny said.

"So, let's milk it," Maeve said.

"You up for going by the 76 station, Sparrow?" Johnny asked.

"Sure." Sparrow found the idea of going to the 76 station particularly enticing since part of her plan for the day included stopping there, and now she didn't need an excuse, but she had to ask Maeve and Johnny something. "Do you think I can ask your uncle Mason about being my daddy yet?"

"NO!" Maeve and Johnny shouted together.

Sparrow wanted to be loyal to Maeve and Johnny, but she felt time ticking away. With the Boy missing, Mama refusing to show herself, and the house up for sale, she didn't have too much of it left. "Any idea when it might be okay?"

"Soon," Johnny said.

"By Saturday," Maeve stated confidently.

"You can't promise Sparrow that. We don't even have it yet," Johnny said.

"But we will. We've got a plan." Maeve looked practically devilish.

"Have what?" Sparrow asked.

"The most perfect, indisputable, bona fide proof that our uncle is your daddy," Maeve said.

Sparrow stopped walking. "Seriously?"

"Yep, more serious than a snakebite," Maeve said.

Sparrow looked at Johnny.

He looked a bit nervous but smiled. He nodded and stuffed his hands into his pockets. "We do."

"Wow." Sparrow let it sink in. She'd liked the idea from the start, but now that it was real and not just a possibility, Sparrow let herself truly believe it. The idea took hold like a kite in the wind, and Sparrow's spirit soared. A daddy didn't replace Mama, but it gave her something she thought she'd lost forever—a parent. The wonderful thing about Mason was that she not only got him but a whole, huge family as a bonus. No one would call her an orphan again.

A heron croaked, and the three kids looked up. A massive white bird flew overhead. They watched it until it was out of sight and then walked on.

"You're sure by Saturday?" Sparrow asked.

"Absolutely," Maeve said.

"That's good. I need a daddy sooner rather than later."

"Why's that?"

"My aunt. She is going to sell the house."

"WHAT!"

"Yep, she put a sign up yesterday."

"That can't happen. A Dalton needs to live in that house."

"I know, but she's determined. She hates it."

"Course she does. It's haunted."

Funny, Sparrow had never considered Dalton House haunted before, but now that Maeve said it, she supposed that's exactly what it was.

"If I didn't know about your ghost and that he was friendly, I'd be scared out of my britches if I lived in your house."

"I guess," Sparrow said. She didn't like being pushed to feel empathetic toward Auntie Geraldine. "With the Boy gone, I have this sick feeling that if the house sells before he gets back, he might not find me if I am not living at Dalton House. I thought if your uncle Mason knew Auntie Geraldine is selling the house, he'd come live there with me. That way I wouldn't have to leave, and the Boy would always be able to find me." *Mama too*, Sparrow thought.

Maeve stopped in the road and put her hands on her hips. "I planned you would come live with us. I mean, it's lonely over at your place. And you know, it's creepy. No offense. Why would you want to stay there?"

Sparrow thought of all the reasons why she'd want to stay at Dalton House—Mama, the Boy, the marsh, her porch, her memories—all of it wrapped up into the bundle she called home.

Johnny came to her rescue. "Of course she wants to live at her house, and I'm sure Uncle Mason would love it there too. He's real handy, so he could fix some of the things Sparrow and her mama weren't able to keep up with. I think it sounds perfect."

Maeve looked dubious.

"He's living in a rusted trailer now, Maeve," Johnny said.

"It's not what I had in mind, but I want to see what this ghost can do, so I suppose you can live there," Maeve conceded.

"The only thing is, I think he'll need to buy it from Auntie Geraldine," Sparrow said.

Maeve and Johnny shared a look Sparrow couldn't read.

"I know Uncle Mason. Once the secret is out about you being his daughter, he'll do what needs to be done," Johnny said.

"Why do you think he hasn't told anyone yet? Hasn't told me?" Sparrow asked.

"I don't think he can. I'm not sure, exactly. But it must have something to do with your auntie Geraldine."

Figured. Auntie Geraldine didn't want Sparrow to have anything. "Why do you think that?"

"Uncle Mason's been spending a lot of time with Wesley Monroe, and your auntie Geraldine has been there too."

"What do you think it means?"

Maeve started to speak, but Johnny put his hand on his sister's arm to stop her. "We've said enough already. We're just guessing right now. Let's get the proof first. We'll fill you in on everything else Saturday."

Sparrow trusted Maeve and Johnny. "As long as you promise to tell me everything."

"We will," Johnny said.

"You're going to change your name, right?" Maeve asked, changing the subject.

Sparrow hadn't thought about it, but now that Maeve mentioned it, she assumed that Mason would change his last name to Dalton. "Wouldn't he want to be a Dalton like me?"

"But you'll be a Casto," Maeve said.

"Dalton or Casto, Sparrow is family. You know better than anyone it's the person, not the name, that matters," Johnny said.

Maeve rolled her eyes. "Not in this town."

Sparrow heard the hurt and felt bad. It'd taken the fight and the picture to bring them together. She'd never tried to befriend Maeve before because it never occurred to her that Maeve would accept her. In truth, Maeve might not have, but all this dividing of families and people were lines drawn in the sand, not a real thing.

"Maeve," Sparrow said, but Maeve didn't hear her.

The 76 station had come into view, and at the sight of it, Maeve dashed ahead, yelling, "Uncle Mason!"

Johnny shrugged apologetically and picked up his pace.

Sparrow matched her stride to Johnny's, and soon they were standing in front of the 76 station.

Mason Casto looked up from the truck he worked on.

Maeve ran straight toward him at top speed.

He put down the huge wrench he held. "Whoa, slow down there, Missy!"

Maeve skidded to a stop.

Mason held up his hand and Maeve high-fived him. Then they engaged in an elaborate handshake that ended with Maeve bumping her hip against his.

"Do they greet each other like that all the time?" Sparrow asked Johnny.

"Not always, but enough to be annoying. Uncle Mason adores Maeve."

Sparrow felt a twinge of jealousy at hearing that. She hoped Mason would adore her someday.

Johnny sauntered up to his uncle and Sparrow followed.

"Look who we found." Maeve pointed proudly at Sparrow.

Sparrow wanted to correct Maeve and remind her that she was the one who found them, *spying*, but Maeve was already talking again.

"We're about half dead with thirst and hoping for some Cokes."

"Is this so?" Mason asked. He slapped Johnny on the back in greeting. "You too?"

Johnny nodded. "I am fairly parched."

"Sparrow, how about you?" Mason didn't pat her on the back or high-five her. He just smiled kindly and said, "Would you like a Coke too?"

"Yes, please." Sparrow's mouth started to water at just

the thought of the sweet, bubbly liquid. There were few things better than an ice-cold Coke on a boiling hot day.

Mason got them all Cokes and one for himself too. He took a swig. "All right, off with you three now. I've got work to do."

"Wait, Uncle Mason. Aren't you forgetting something?" Maeve put her hand on her uncle's arm to keep him from turning away.

A perplexed look came over his face.

"You know, about the party," Maeve prompted, raising her eyebrows exaggeratedly high.

He still looked befuddled.

"You know, the family cookout? You said we should invite . . ." Maeve used her thumb to point at Sparrow.

"Oh, right!" He slapped himself on the head. "We're having a gathering at our place on Saturday. We'd like it if you'd stop by."

"A *family* gathering," Maeve said.

"Mostly family, but the Monroes are coming too," Mason said.

"What! You didn't tell me that! Blah." Maeve pretended to gag.

"You will be on your best behavior and be nice to those kids."

"They're so snotty," Maeve whined.

"I mean it. Wesley's been helping me out with some-thing important, and you'll show them every courtesy, or you can miss the party."

Maeve crossed her arms. "Fine. But they better not start something."

He pointed a grease-stained finger in Maeve's face. "You better not start something."

"I won't if they won't," Maeve answered, putting her hands on her hips.

"Maeve, I mean it. You'll be nice."

Sparrow sighed. She figured this back and forth could go on all day, so she interrupted before Maeve could say that the Monroes better be nice. "I'd love to come, thank you."

"It will be good to have you. I don't think we've had a Dalton out our way since way back when your mama and I used to pal around together as kids."

Maeve, Johnny, and Sparrow shared a meaningful look.

Mason looked at them curiously, but only said, "Bring your auntie Geraldine too, if she wants to come."

The kids stood there awkwardly, not knowing what to say. Not one of them wanted Auntie Geraldine at the cookout.

Mason laughed. "Geraldine's not that bad. She's just misunderstood."

Maeve gave her uncle a look that said what all three of them were thinking without uttering one word.

Mason shook his head. "Remind me never to get on y'all's bad side. All right, you three. Get on out of here. That truck is not going to fix itself."

Sparrow, Maeve, and Johnny left, sipping their Cokes. As soon as they were a few paces away, Maeve nudged Sparrow with her elbow. "You're coming to a Casto *family* party."

Sparrow smiled. Yes, she was. Everything would be okay after all.

CHAPTER SEVENTEEN

Sparrow practically floated home. Everything was coming together. She no longer needed to worry about Dalton House being sold or living with Auntie Geraldine. By Saturday, Mason Casto would be her daddy, and they'd live in Dalton House together. Auntie Geraldine would go back to Havisham where she belonged, and Sparrow would be left in peace to solve the mystery of the Boy, and most important, get Mama back.

Sparrow still didn't know where the Boy had gone or understand what kept him away, but finding the gravestone gave her hope. The more she thought about the way the swirling spirits acted, the more convinced she became that it meant something important. She was on the right path. She just had to keep following it.

Sparrow walked past the FOR SALE sign. It still lay askew in the dirt where she'd left it, and the sight of it filled her with glee. It felt like a good omen.

When she entered the kitchen, Auntie Geraldine was pulling a chicken and rice casserole out of the oven. The rich, warm scent made the house smell like a bouquet of memories. Sparrow leaned against the kitchen door and watched Auntie Geraldine work. The radio still played softly in the background. A country singer crooned "Will the Circle Be Unbroken" in the lonesome way that they do, and Sparrow closed her eyes, conjuring up Mama in Auntie Geraldine's place.

At the funeral, someone told Sparrow her memories would fade with time. This was true for some, but other recollections of Mama were so vivid, merely invoking the thought of her summoned her with a clarity that knocked the breath out of Sparrow.

She heard the sound of two dinner plates being set on the table and opened her eyes. Auntie Geraldine sat in Mama's chair.

Reluctantly, Sparrow went to her usual place. "The radio was on when I left this morning."

"I know," Auntie Geraldine said. "I like hearing it play."

Sparrow felt she could be more generous toward Auntie Geraldine now that she knew she wouldn't have to live with her forever, and she let herself imagine what it was like for Auntie Geraldine to miss so many people. She'd lost her husband, all the older Daltons, and now Mama.

Mama once told Sparrow Auntie Geraldine was lonely, and that was why she was so prickly. *Prickly* was Mama's word, not Sparrow's. Sparrow had different words to describe Auntie Geraldine. Even so, Sparrow wondered if Auntie Geraldine did feel lonely.

"Where'd you go today?" Auntie Geraldine opened her napkin and spread it across her lap.

"Outside, like I said in my note."

"Outside, huh? Did you go to town?"

"You told me I couldn't." Sparrow dug her fork into the steaming casserole and lifted it to her mouth.

"I find that interesting considering I saw you at the 76 station drinking Cokes with those Casto kids and that filthy mechanic." Auntie Geraldine's mouth drew into a thin line and her face hardened, and just like that, Mama's version of the lonely Auntie Geraldine vanished and Sparrow's version of her—the mean, unmovable one—appeared.

She didn't know why it had to be like this. They might be friends if Auntie Geraldine would let them. Sparrow set her fork down. She no longer felt like eating. "The 76 station doesn't count. It isn't *in* town. It's before it."

Daylight moved toward twilight, casting the usually sunny kitchen into shadows.

Auntie Geraldine pushed her chair back and stood. As she moved, her shadow arched and morphed until it eclipsed the room. "You've disobeyed me for the last time."

Sparrow stood too. She didn't need to be afraid of Auntie Geraldine anymore. Mason Casto was going to be her daddy and she would tell him to ban Auntie Geraldine from Dalton House. Maybe even Beulah. She heard the crush of salt as she pushed her chair back. "I didn't disobey you. The 76 station isn't in town. It's before it. What's wrong with town anyway?"

"The Castos. They're trouble. Fighting and carrying on like they have no manners. Your mama always loved hanging out with that Mason, and look what it got her."

"*Me?*" Sparrow asked, feeling emboldened.

For a moment, Auntie Geraldine looked shaken. Then she slid back to her normal, mean self. "He changed your mama. He rubbed the Dalton right off her, and I'll not have them do the same to you. You don't have enough of it to lose."

A fire ignited in Sparrow's belly. "Don't you talk about my mama. She was a better Dalton than you."

Auntie Geraldine ignored Sparrow and strode across the kitchen to the phone. She punched in a number. "Mason. This is Geraldine."

Sparrow's mouth went dry. Auntie Geraldine had no right to call Mason. The Castos were hers.

Auntie Geraldine looked at Sparrow as she spoke. "It's about my niece. She's being punished. She's not allowed to leave the property and I saw her today at the gas station with some of your kin."

Sparrow heard the deep tenor of Mason's voice cut Auntie Geraldine off, but she was too far away to make out his words. She hoped he was telling Auntie Geraldine to stop picking on her.

"Yes. Yes. That's not the point," Auntie Geraldine said curtly. "Please let them know they are not to socialize with Sparrow. If she shows up at your place of work or home, I expect you to send her away."

Auntie Geraldine became silent, but she squeezed the phone so tight the tips of her fingers turned white. Sparrow wondered if Mason was telling Auntie Geraldine that he was her father.

After a rather long pause, Auntie Geraldine snapped, "It is not up to you to raise my niece. I'll do what I see fit, and I expect you to respect my wishes."

Mason's voice resonated from the other end of the line. Sparrow hoped Mason was telling Auntie Geraldine that she had no right to raise Sparrow at all and he was coming to claim her. Maybe he'd get in his truck and drive over tonight.

"Thank you. Glad you understand. Good night." Auntie Geraldine smiled smugly and hung up the phone. "Go over there and he'll send you home. He's agreed to tell Maeve and Johnny to stay away from you too."

Sparrow felt like she was sinking. She'd hung all her hopes on Maeve, Johnny, and Mason. In one phone call, Auntie Geraldine had bashed her dreams to pieces. Sparrow felt like a dinghy trying to survive a hurricane. "Why would you do that? Those are my friends."

Auntie Geraldine spoke with triumphant confidence. "You'll learn who's in charge one way or the other. I've already managed to make this house more livable, and I'll make you easier to live with too."

Sparrow narrowed her eyes at Auntie Geraldine. She wondered what else Auntie Geraldine had planned. "What do you mean?"

"You and I are done talking. Go to your room. Now."

Sparrow supposed they were done talking. She had nothing to say to Auntie Geraldine. She didn't want to speak to her ever again.

Sparrow climbed the stairs, each step like a plodding slog up a steep slope. Her body felt like lead.

When she got to the top of the steps, she paused at Mama's door. She hadn't been in her room since she died. Sparrow wondered if it would smell like Mama. Feel like her. She missed Mama so much. She wanted to be close to her again.

She pushed open the door.

Shock engulfed her. The room was bare. The bed stripped.

Sparrow ran into the room and pulled open Mama's dresser drawers. Empty. Empty. Empty. She slammed each drawer closed with an unrelenting force.

She yanked open the closet. Empty. She kicked it closed.

Nothing of Mama remained.

She had been wiped away.

Auntie Geraldine stomped up the stairs. "What in the world is all that racket?"

"Where's Mama's stuff?"

"Donated it."

"Donated to who?"

"The church, of course. That's what you do when someone dies."

"You *erased* her."

"Don't be overly dramatic. I did what needed to be done. Waiting wouldn't have made it easier. You couldn't have expected me to move all your mama's stuff to my house. There's no place to put it."

"I'll never live with you at your house."

"You don't have a choice. Dalton House has been sold."

"I hate you."

"I'm not very fond of you either." Auntie Geraldine turned on her heels and went into her bedroom, slamming the door shut behind her.

The tears arrived so fast and so hard that Sparrow's breath came in ragged, body-wrenching gulps. She didn't understand Auntie Geraldine at all. She had no heart.

Sparrow gently pulled Mama's door closed.

She went to her bedroom and locked the door. She sat on the seat under the window that looked out over the marsh. The window was open, and Sparrow rested her head on the sill. She felt a grainy substance under her arms. More salt. At any other time, Sparrow would have investigated the salt, but all the curiosity, all the struggle had gone right out of her. Auntie Geraldine had won.

Sparrow stared at the marsh and sought comfort from it. The waxing moon had risen bright as a beacon, flooding the night with light, and the entire nighttime vista was hers to view as if it were day. She saw the oak trees dripping with moss, the reed grass silhouetted against the dark sky, and something else too.

Sparrow sat up.

The Boy walked across the marsh in the moonlight.

CHAPTER EIGHTEEN

Sparrow grabbed her gum boots from her closet and crept into the hallway. The house was dark except for a small sliver of light shining under Auntie Geraldine's door. Auntie Geraldine had gone to her room, but she was not asleep yet.

Sparrow clutched her boots to her chest and inched down the stairs. Dalton House was an old building with creaky bones, and every step brought a moan of complaint. The world around Sparrow was so mouse quiet, it felt like the house was yelling at her.

She was halfway down the steps when she heard Auntie Geraldine walking overhead. She pressed her body against the wall, seeking the shadows.

Auntie Geraldine opened her bedroom door, and light flowed onto the landing.

Sparrow slid down the wall, crouching into the darkest part of the stairs.

Auntie Geraldine called out, "Sparrow?"

Sparrow's heart beat like a hummingbird's.

Auntie Geraldine stepped into the hallway, the hem of her white nightgown peeking out of her pink housecoat. "Sparrow?"

Sparrow clasped her hand over her mouth to keep from answering.

Auntie Geraldine looked at Sparrow's door. It was shut with no light coming from beneath it. She scanned the hallway and then withdrew inside her room, shutting the door.

Sparrow counted twenty Mississippis before moving again. When she did, she stayed low, half crawling, half sliding down the rest of the stairs, her heart still beating like it wished to take flight.

She reached the bottom and scrutinized the front door, unsure of her ability to open it without alerting Auntie Geraldine. If the stairs grumbled, the front door shrieked like a banshee.

Sparrow shifted her gum boots to a more secure hold and considered her options. She spied the window and tiptoed toward it. It stood about waist high and led to the front porch. That was her way out.

She inched the lock open and gingerly coaxed the window up just enough for her to crawl through. She put her hand on the sill and a grainy substance prickled her palm. She paused, examining it. A thin line of white sand-like grains lined the window. She picked up a few grains and rubbed them between her fingers, then tasted them. More salt.

Salt seemed to be everywhere these days. It was odd, but she didn't have time to sort it out now. She didn't want to risk the Boy leaving. She brushed the salt off the sill and scooched onto the porch.

Her next obstacle was the screen door. Though it usually slammed shut loudly, it mostly did so because Sparrow wanted it to. If she treated it gently, it responded in kind.

She eased it opened and squeezed out. Then held on to the door, guiding it closed until she heard the soft brush of lumber against lumber.

She jumped from the front steps and landed softly in the grass. She pulled on her gum boots and sprinted across the lawn, her bare feet flopping around in the boots as she ran.

Her escape from the house had taken longer than she'd wanted and she was afraid the Boy would be gone, but when she reached the water's edge, he was still there. He waded waist-deep in the water at the center of the marsh. His form glowed in the moonlight like a luminous fish. He wandered to and fro as if lost, repeating the pattern of his steps over and over, like a movie scene being rewound and replayed.

Sparrow shuddered.

She'd never been afraid of the Boy before, but now he looked positively ghostly. The sight chilled her to the bone, and she wondered what had happened to him.

She took a tentative step toward him and her foot sank into the moist, spongy soil. She felt tepid water flow over the top of her boot and took a second tentative step. Both feet descended into the mud, and she felt the downward pull of the sucking silt.

She paused, suddenly hyperaware of her surroundings.

On the far bank, the mangrove trees grew in thick clumps, their shadowy forms silent sentinels guarding the ancient ecosystem. All around her, frogs wailed their deafening song and animals hunted. Folks assumed the marsh slept at night because that's when people did, but the marsh was a nocturnal creature. It rested during the day, lazily basking in the sun. At night, it sprang to life.

Sparrow swallowed, nervous.

Though it was a cloudless night and she could see surprisingly well, the animals she most needed to respect wore the water like a cloak. Practically invisible, gators and cottonmouths glided through the marsh, barely making a ripple, their black eyes skimming the surface of the water. Either could be an inch from her, and she wouldn't know it unless they wanted her to.

Despite her fear, she took another step toward the Boy. She needed to go to him. This was the first time she'd seen him since they'd promised to help each other, and she had to find a way to reach him. Not only was the Boy her link to Mama, he was her friend and he needed help. He needed Sparrow.

She took another step and then halted. A few feet in front of her, the water moved, and fear shot through her like a bolt of lightning.

She took a slow, deliberate step backward.

The hair on her neck prickled and out of the corner of her eye, she saw more movement. She froze. Then slowly turned her head. Passing before her was something so rare she'd assumed the tales and stories of it were pure myth.

Twenty feet from Sparrow, a tawny Florida panther strode across the marsh, trailed by her spotted cub. Each stealthy step the panthers took showcased the rippled muscle and the unsurpassed strength that cemented their sovereignty over all other creatures.

Sparrow held her pose, fighting the urge to flee. She knew better than to run from a predator. Sleek and sinewy, the panther lived by instinct. If Sparrow ran, the panther would chase, and her slight child's body would offer no protection against the speed and might of the great cat.

The panther and her baby strode leisurely through the marsh, the tall grasses bowing before them.

Behind the cats, the Boy continued his ghostly pantomime unnoticed.

The kitten mewed. The panther turned, licked his fur, and nudged him forward.

When the panthers got parallel to Sparrow, they looked her way and growled, the baby's bleat a weak imitation of his mother's menacing snarl.

In all her life, Sparrow had never felt such primal fear. Her instinct railed against her reason, demanding she run. It took all she had to stay rooted in place.

The mother panther raised her lips, her teeth glinting in the moonlight. She growled another low warning and pushed her kitten in front of her. They moved on, taking their time, their rule of the land uncontested. The nighttime marsh was meant for panthers and ghosts, not girls. Sparrow wondered how she ever let herself believe she had sprung to life from the swamp. The swamp existed unto itself, and Auntie Geraldine's warnings of the dangers of the marsh echoed in Sparrow's memory. She suppressed a shudder.

When the cats were far enough away that they were mere shadows in the dark, Sparrow took one slow step back, then another, until she was close enough to the house to run for the door.

She flew through the screen door, adrenaline surging through her veins. It creaked, pushed to the limit of its hinges, and then started its journey home. Sparrow lunged for it, catching it before it slammed closed. She didn't need to go from one close call to another.

She slipped out of her boots, climbed back through the window, and eased it shut. Only a few hours earlier she felt everything coming together. Now it all slid away.

Sparrow crept up the steps to her room, where she could view the marsh in safety. She went to the window and looked out. The mythical Florida panther was gone, but the Boy was there. He still wandered to and fro as if lost, playing and replaying his scene in the moonlight.

CHAPTER NINETEEN

Sparrow watched the Boy from her window. She hoped to find clues to unravel the mystery of his unexpected departure and unnerving return, but he only repeated the same ghostly pantomime over and over again, leaving her worried and confused. When she reluctantly went to bed, she fell into a deep sleep filled with swamp-tinged dreams of ghosts and panthers.

The next morning, she awoke later than usual to a sun-soaked room.

The sound of Auntie Geraldine's footsteps on the hardwood downstairs broke through the haze of sleepiness and reminded Sparrow of all she had gained and lost the day before—the Boy, her chance to bring Mama back, Dalton House, Maeve, Johnny, Mason. All of it, Auntie Geraldine's fault. Each time she thought Auntie Geraldine had done her worst, she found a new way to torment Sparrow.

Auntie Geraldine didn't call Sparrow down for breakfast. If she had, Sparrow wouldn't have gone. She never wanted to see or speak to her again. Auntie Geraldine said she'd find something that Sparrow loved and rip it to shreds. True to her words, Auntie Geraldine had done just that. She'd given away all of Mama's belongings, sold Dalton House, and told the Castos to stay away from her. Auntie Geraldine had done more than find one thing Sparrow loved. She'd found everything, except the Boy.

At the thought of the Boy, a new wave of anguish washed over Sparrow. His disappearance and ghostly return tormented her. She didn't know how or why the Boy had turned into a shade of his former self, but she refused to be robbed of him too. He was her only link to Mama, her only friend. Sparrow was headed for a hard life with Auntie Geraldine in Havisham, and she couldn't bear it alone.

Sparrow went to her opened window and leaned out. Under her palms she felt a gritty substance, but she didn't bother to look at it. She already knew it was salt. The entire house was awash with the stuff.

From her window, Sparrow looked down upon the covered porch and the long stretch of marsh that made up Dalton land. Her land. The night before, she'd almost let herself forget how much she loved it.

Gingerly, she put one leg over the ledge. Then the other, and sat on the sill. Just to the left of her window, her favorite oak tree dripped with Spanish moss. It was a tall, broad beauty with thick, wide branches that reached toward her like arms.

Sparrow leaped.

The oak caught her, and Sparrow shimmied down its trunk to the ground.

Under the sun's caress, the marsh had turned friendly again. It called to Sparrow and, obediently, she answered.

The tide was out. Forlorn puddles dotted the watershed, and the sandbar stretched all the way to the horizon.

At the bank, Sparrow sank her bare feet into the silty sand. It felt good to let her feet descend into the rich, velvety mud. It squished between her toes and covered the tops of her feet, sucking her down until it wrapped around her ankles.

She made her way to where the Boy stood the night before. Each step of her journey a fight against the pull of the marsh mud. Birds scattered and hermit crabs scampered as she walked deeper and deeper into their world.

When she reached her destination, she tried to view it from the Boy's perspective. Behind her, Dalton House sat on the marsh's northern bank. Beulah was to the south, about a mile away, and to the west and east of where she stood, the sandbar cut a path to the sea.

Between the darkness and the distance, it had been hard to tell which direction the Boy walked the night before.

She couldn't decide if he had walked toward Dalton House, town, or the sea. Each direction had different possibilities and likely different meanings. His reason for being in the marsh was a mystery. A mystery she needed to solve quickly if she had any hope of getting the Boy and Mama back before she no longer lived at Dalton House.

The thought of saying goodbye to Dalton House and the marsh on top of what she'd already lost made Sparrow feel as forlorn as a whip-poor-will. As if sensing her anguish, the marsh sent a breeze that tickled the reed grass. The grass bowed and kissed the backs of her palms.

Sparrow smiled at the marsh's playfulness and allowed the delights of the marsh to soothe her. For the rest of the morning, she caught hermit crabs and let their feet tickle the palm of her hand before releasing them into their muddy homes. She watched tiny fish swim in the puddles left behind by the tide, and egrets silently stalk their prey. When she felt the tide start to rise and water, instead of mud, crest over her feet, she headed back to shore.

As was typical with the marsh, she had wandered farther and deeper than she realized. By the time she made it back, the water touched her ankles, and the little fish swam freely, no longer trapped in the tidal pools.

Exhausted from her excursion, Sparrow nestled up to an oak tree to watch the tide rise from the safety of shore. She admired the way the light slowly shifted as the sun moved across the sky and the way the marsh gradually changed as the water rose.

As she sat watching the marsh, Sparrow thought about the way the Boy looked in the moonlight. He had wandered to and fro as if lost, repeating the pattern of his steps over and over, like a movie scene being rewound and replayed.

Suddenly, Sparrow jumped up. She knew what the Boy had been doing in the marsh. He didn't wander back and forth because he was lost.

He was looking for something.

CHAPTER TWENTY

Sparrow ran toward the house. When she got close, she crouched down to keep from being seen from the living room window. She crept up to it and peeked in. Auntie Geraldine sat on the couch, reading through a thick packet of papers. She was busy. *Thank goodness*, Sparrow thought.

She tiptoed upstairs, opened the door to her bedroom, and nearly jumped out of her skin. Maeve, Johnny, and Elena sat on her bed.

"Took you long enough," Maeve said.

"Holy palmetto bug. Y'all nearly scared the life out of me. What are y'all doing here? I mean, how are you here?"

Maeve grinned like the devil. "Which do you want first? The how or the what?"

"Either." Sparrow wanted to run across the room and sweep all three kids up in a bear hug. She'd thought she would never see her friends again, and now Maeve, Johnny, and Elena were in her room.

"The how. Easy-peasy." Maeve pointed to the open window.

"Not for me. That was a first," Elena said. "I've been up and down fire escapes lots of times, but I've never climbed a tree into a window before. I don't think I've climbed a tree ever." Elena seemed pleased with herself.

"She needs more practice," Maeve said. "She almost got us caught."

"But I didn't," Elena said smugly. She looked happier today. She also looked different. Not as different as the last time Sparrow had seen her, but not like the fortune-teller Sparrow had first met either. Her chestnut hair was down, and she wore some jewelry, but not as much as she had that first day. She also wore shorts instead of a sundress.

"Okay, so *why* are y'all here? Don't get me wrong, you three are a sight for sore eyes, but did your uncle tell you what Auntie Geraldine said?" Sparrow asked.

"He did. That's why we're here," Maeve said.

"And because we've got some news," Johnny added.

Maeve leaned close to Sparrow, and for a split second she thought Maeve was going to hug her. Instead, she sniffed her.

Sparrow pushed her away. "What in the world are you doing?"

"You smell different. You used to smell like roses, slightly rotten. Not bad exactly, but kind of creepy. It

174

reminded me of a grave. Now you don't. You smell like normal kid."

Sometimes Maeve was too honest. "Um, well . . ." Sparrow didn't know how to respond to that observation.

"That is exactly what I thought the first time I met her!" Elena shoved Maeve playfully, and the two girls smiled at each other knowingly.

Sparrow lifted her hand to her nose.

"I said you didn't smell that way now," Maeve reminded Sparrow. "Come to think of it. Your house feels different. It feels normal too. Less haunted house and more Beulah. Maybe it's all this yellow."

Sparrow looked around her room and saw it through Maeve's eyes. Mama had painted it the color of buttercups and bought pillows to match. "My mama picked it. She said it was cheery."

"It is," Johnny said helpfully.

"I didn't say it wasn't. I just said it was normal. I don't know. I kind of expected you to live in a different sort of room. You know, something a little more"—Maeve indicated Sparrow's overall appearance—"fitting."

"Maeve!" Johnny said.

"*What?* If you said I looked like a carrot, I wouldn't argue with you. Look at my hair. It's just who I am. I might punch you in the face, but I wouldn't argue."

175

"You *punch* people?" Elena's brows knitted with concern as if she just realized she was holding a poisonous coral snake instead of its friendly cousin, the king snake.

The three Beulah kids laughed.

"Only the ones she doesn't like," Johnny said reassuringly.

"Don't worry, I like you," Maeve said, jabbing Elena in the ribs.

Elena shot Sparrow a dubious look.

Sparrow chuckled, and as she watched the three kids she realized Maeve had a point. Each of them had a distinctive look. Maeve and Johnny had the Casto red hair. Elena looked like her uncle. Sparrow looked, well, she looked like herself. Actually, she looked a little like Elena. But the way they looked didn't matter. They looked the way they did because that's the way they'd been born. It didn't make them one thing or the other. Dandelions and roses looked vastly different, but they were both flowers.

"So, besides defying my aunt, why are y'all here?"

"After we heard about your aunt's call, we knew you'd have a hard time following up on the gravestone, so we went to see Elena for you."

Sparrow turned to Elena. "Did you come up with a new theory?"

Elena gathered her long hair and drew it over one shoulder. Her enviable cascade of waves fell perfectly in place. "Nope, but I talked to Eli."

"I thought he doesn't believe in mystical stuff," Sparrow said, recalling their conversation.

"He doesn't. But he is a history professor."

"What does that have to do with ghosts?" Sparrow asked.

"If someone is going to have advice on how to figure out who's buried in that unmarked grave, it's him," Elena said.

"We've come to break you out and take you to Eli," Maeve said.

"She's not in jail, Maeve," Johnny said.

"Might as well be. Have you met her aunt?"

Johnny sighed. "You don't have to say everything that comes into your head."

"Yes, I do. Otherwise it spills out anyway."

Sparrow watched the two siblings bicker. Even though they squabbled, the comfort and ease with which they spoke to each other showcased their closeness rather than the divide caused by their argument. Maeve and Johnny loved each other in that fierce way that only family can.

"Should we break this up?" Elena asked Sparrow.

"Definitely." Sparrow remembered Maeve's performance with Mason. She could argue all day.

Elena motioned to Maeve and Johnny to wrap it up and the two bracelets she wore clinked together softly. "Should we go?"

"Yes," Maeve said, glaring at her brother.

Johnny just smiled and shrugged before climbing out the window.

Elena, Sparrow, and Maeve followed him out, and before Sparrow knew it she was running across the marsh she loved with three friends by her side.

CHAPTER TWENTY-ONE

By the time they reached the flea market, the kids were hot, tired, and out of breath. Along the way, Sparrow had filled them in on seeing the Boy in the marsh the night before and told them about her encounter with the panther. Throughout the telling, Maeve looked enthralled, Elena pensive, and Johnny sympathetic.

As they wove their way through the vendor stalls, Sparrow said, "I think the Boy is looking for something in the marsh."

Maeve paused at the faux fur coat seller and took a pink one off the rack. She slipped it on and posed. "That makes sense. You see that kind of stuff in movies all the time."

Sparrow watched Maeve preen. "I don't think we watch the same kind of movies."

Elena nodded her head approvingly at Maeve's outfit. "I think you need these to complete the look." Elena pulled off her big sunglasses and put them on Maeve.

Maeve modeled her getup.

"You look like a movie star," Sparrow said.

"I foresee fame in your future," Elena pronounced theatrically.

Maeve laughed and returned the coat to the rack. "Let's hope so. I'd love to be famous." She draped her arms around Elena's and Sparrow's shoulders and ushered them forward. The three girls walked along like that, tripping each other up and giggling, until they came to a used bookseller.

Johnny stopped abruptly and started rummaging through a box of books. "Back to our earlier conversation, I'd trust what Maeve says about movies. She's an expert. She watches a lot of television."

Elena walked to Johnny and picked up a novel for sale. "So you're the book expert and she's the TV expert?"

"Pretty much." Johnny smirked and flipped through pages of a thick paperback.

If they continued at their present pace, it would be nightfall before they made it to Eli's antiquities booth. When they left Dalton house, Sparrow had still been raw with anger at Auntie Geraldine for calling Mason and telling him to keep his family away from her. Now, though, as she walked along in the sunshine, relishing the time with her new friends, her anger had been supplanted by growing unease. She would get in big trouble if Auntie Geraldine noticed her missing. As far as Auntie Geraldine knew, Sparrow was in her room pouting. She hoped Auntie Geraldine would be too mad to check on her. She probably would, but still . . . as much as she was enjoying herself, they should move faster.

"We better keep moving," Sparrow said.

"Agreed." Maeve grabbed Johnny by the collar and pulled him away from the vendor. "But if you let him get distracted by books, we'll never get anywhere."

Elena put down the novel she held and followed the kids.

Sparrow waited for Elena to catch up and then fell into step beside her. "What do I do when I find what the Boy is looking for?"

"Give it back to him, of course," Elena said.

"But he's a ghost. He can't hold stuff," Maeve said indignantly. Sparrow thought Maeve had a good point.

"It's *symbolic*, obviously." Elena kind of sounded like she was bickering with Maeve, but neither girl showed any signs of animosity. Rather, they seemed to enjoy matching wits. The two girls kept bantering, and by the time Eli's booth came into view, Maeve and Elena had moved on from discussing ghosts to arguing about the probability of aliens.

Sparrow left the girls to their debate, choosing instead to walk next to Johnny in harmonious silence. Johnny was easy to be around. He didn't require Sparrow to be anything other than herself. After weeks of living with Auntie Geraldine, she found it a relief to be near someone like him.

When Eli saw the kids approach, he set aside the book he was reading, *Orphan Trains: Small Towns, Big Hearts*. It was the same book the Monroes were selling for charity at church. The one Mr. Monroe wrote. "Well, this is a nice surprise."

"Hey, Eli. Sorry, I'm not reading fortunes today." The doors to Elena's purple tent were shut and a sign that read BACK SOON was pinned to the fabric.

Eli stood up. "Doesn't matter to me, kiddo. The trip was my idea, but the fortune-telling was yours, remember?"

Sparrow, Maeve, and Johnny looked at Elena curiously, but Elena didn't offer any extra details on her fortune-telling business, and the three Beulah kids were too polite to ask after private affairs.

Elena pointed to the kids. "You remember Maeve and Johnny from this morning. And you know Sparrow."

Eli adjusted his geeky-chic glasses. "Of course. Good to see you all again. Sparrow, I'll have your watch back by Saturday. Think you can stop by to pick it up?"

"Sure." Sparrow had forgotten all about the watch.

Maeve squinted at Sparrow, clearly wanting to know what Eli was talking about.

"Tell you later," Sparrow said to Maeve.

"Can I help you kids with something?" Eli asked.

"We were wondering if we could ask you some questions about historical research," Elena said.

Eli pretended to swoon. "Be still my heart."

Elena laughed and playfully swatted at her uncle. "Be serious, Eli."

"Of course. Grab some chairs and gather round. I'm a fountain of information." Eli bowed grandly.

Sparrow wondered if Eli had been the one to inspire Elena's dramatic side, and it made her curious about which of her traits she had inherited from her father. Once she had Mason, she would be able to find out. That is, if Mason still wanted her after what Auntie Geraldine had done. She had been waiting for the right time to ask Maeve and Johnny about the plan for telling him that he was her father, but she hadn't found it yet.

The kids grabbed chairs and set them up in a circle so they could chat.

"Elena told you about my research on childhood in New York City at the turn of the century?"

"Um . . . no." Sparrow didn't understand half of what Eli just said. "She only mentioned that you were a history professor, and knew a lot about research."

Eli shot Elena a pretend injured look.

Elena rolled her eyes. "Oh, *please*." She turned to Maeve,

Johnny, and Sparrow for sympathy. "You have no idea what it's like to live with a pack of academics. Someone is always either working on a book or reading a book. It's impossible to keep up."

"Sounds like my kind of household," Johnny said.

Maeve groaned. "Not mine. I'm with Elena. Living with Johnny is bad enough."

Eli chuckled.

"What about your grandmother?" Sparrow asked, recalling her conversation with Elena the first day they met. "Is she a professor too?"

Elena looked at her fortune-teller tent. "She died about a year ago."

Eli squeezed Elena's shoulder. "She was a traveling fortune-teller. Elena and I struck out this summer to retrace her footsteps."

Elena turned back to the group and smiled, but her eyelashes were damp. "Anyway, back to *how* to research."

"Yes." Eli slapped his hands on his knees.

Elena told Eli about the gravestone with the missing name and then handed the conversation over to Sparrow.

Eli leaned forward, giving Sparrow his full attention, and she could see the professorial side of his personality. She thought he must be very good at being a professor, even if he didn't look the part.

"Remember how I told you I was looking for someone who lived at my house a long time ago? I'm searching for a boy about ten years old, and I found a gravestone that could be his, but I'm not sure. I don't know the boy's name. And there's no name on the tombstone anyway," Sparrow told Eli.

"Hmm . . . do you have anything else to go on?"

"The gravestone was really worn, but I was able to make out the year of death. 1901," Sparrow said.

"That's a great clue!" Eli said encouragingly. "If I were looking, I'd start with newspapers from that year. Childhood deaths were common then, but Beulah is a small town. It's unlikely more than one ten-year-old died that year. It might have been news. The most important thing when researching is to be open-minded. Sometimes history unravels in unexpected ways once you start digging."

"Where do I find newspapers from 1901?" Sparrow bit her lip. That was ages ago.

"I'd start with the Beulah archives," Eli said.

"What are they?" Sparrow had never heard of the Beulah archives. She thought she knew her town inside and out.

Johnny answered. "A collection of historical documents about a place or a group of people."

"Exactly. You'd make a good history professor," Eli said.

"I'm going to be a lawyer." Johnny's expression had the same hope and determination Sparrow had seen on his older sister's face when she talked about Vanderbilt.

"A more lucrative option, to be sure." Eli smiled. "Anyway, I'd start there, but it might be hard to get access."

"Why?" Maeve asked.

"It's a private collection. Private collectors don't have to share or even show anyone what they have. It's unusual, but it happens. The Beulah collection is difficult to access. I was hoping to have a look there myself, but I haven't been able to get an appointment." Eli adjusted his glasses again.

"Why not?" Sparrow asked.

"The person who owns it doesn't think my uncle is a real scholar because he came to town with the flea market." Elena scoffed. "Can you imagine? Spend five minutes listening to Eli and you know he's the real deal."

"Who are the snobby folks that own this private collection?" Maeve asked.

"The Monroes," Johnny said.

Maeve crossed her arms over her chest. "Figures."

Sparrow had to agree with Maeve. Looking down on Eli because he sold his antiques at the flea market sounded like the Monroes.

Sparrow started to say something comforting to Eli to make him feel better about being snubbed by them, but he got a customer before she could.

Eli left the kids to talk to the shopper about an antique magnifying glass, and the foursome decided it was time to start walking back toward Sparrow's house.

"I told you talking to Eli was a good idea." Elena nudged Sparrow with her elbow, pleased with herself.

Johnny kicked the dirt as they walked. "Checking out the archives is a great idea, but how will you get an appointment?"

"No clue. But I'm going to figure out a way." Once Sparrow knew what the Boy wanted, she would be closer to what she craved—Mama back. Simply thinking about seeing Mama again made Sparrow's insides squishy with anticipation.

"Better you than me. Just the idea of going to the Monroes' gives me hives." Maeve shuddered and rubbed her arms like they were crawling with chiggers.

Maeve, Johnny, and Elena walked with Sparrow to the edge of the marsh and stopped. Sparrow hated the idea of Maeve, Johnny, and Elena leaving, but she understood that they needed to go home. They had families waiting for them.

When it was time to say goodbye, Maeve gave Johnny a knowing look.

Johnny pulled Elena away to show her something in what was obviously a preplanned ruse to let Maeve have a private moment with Sparrow.

Maeve checked to make sure Johnny and Elena were out of earshot and then said, "Everything is all set for Saturday. We've got your proof like we promised."

"Do you still think the family party is a good idea?" All day, Sparrow had been searching for the right opportunity to ask about Mason but it never seemed to come around. Now that they were talking about it, she realized she had been avoiding asking the question because she was afraid of the answer.

"Of course I do," Maeve said with absolute conviction.

"But my auntie Geraldine. She told Mason to turn me away and . . . he agreed." Sparrow looked at the ground. Tears stung her eyes and she didn't want Maeve to feel bad. Maeve and Johnny had been great friends to her. They'd done everything they knew how to do to help her.

"Never mind about that." Maeve waved her hand dismissively. "That was to get your aunt to stop lecturing him. You should have heard him after. Well, Uncle Mason is really nice so he didn't say anything mean. But he said your auntie Geraldine needed to remember what it was like to be a kid and your mama would want her to do right by you. He plans to get you. I know it. Come to the party Saturday and you'll see. You're not an orphan."

"Maeve, we better get going," Johnny called. It was starting to get dark.

"Coming." Maeve began to leave and then turned back. She wrapped Sparrow in a tight hug. "See you Saturday, cousin."

Sparrow squeezed Maeve back. It was the second time she had been hugged since Mama died and both times Maeve had done the hugging. "See you Saturday, cousin."

Maeve dashed over to Elena and Johnny. Sparrow stood at the edge of the marsh and watched the three kids run toward town.

Mama's death had brought her so much sadness, but it had also brought her other things, happier ones—Maeve, Johnny, Elena, a daddy. She wondered why life hadn't let her have all the good things at once.

CHAPTER TWENTY-TWO

Sparrow spent the evening by her bedroom window watching for the Boy and plotting her next move. After the liveliness of spending the day with Maeve, Johnny, and Elena, the emptiness of Dalton House pressed upon her. With each creak of the floor and moan of the rafters, loneliness squeezed Sparrow like an accordion.

She wanted Mama and the Boy back with a fierceness that burned.

To get them back, she needed to help the Boy. That meant learning about his life, so she could figure out what he wanted now that he was a spirit. The Monroes' archives promised the best chance at uncovering information about him. Getting access was the problem. Not only did she need an appointment, she needed to get there. The Monroes lived in a palatial mansion seven miles outside of town. Too far for Sparrow to walk.

Sparrow stayed by the window until late in the evening, planning and waiting for the Boy, but if he wandered the marsh that night, he did so unobserved. Shortly after she got home from the flea market, a fierce thunderstorm rolled into Beulah. High winds drove the rain sideways, and thick, dark clouds blackened the moon. The only thing Sparrow could see from her bedroom window was her reflection staring back at her.

When Sparrow finally allowed herself to sleep, she rested uneasily in a fitful half slumber of strange dreams and pounding rain. The tin roof echoed each falling drop, creating a thunderous drumming instead of the usual soft tapping.

By the time Friday morning rose bright and shining like a freshly scrubbed babe, Sparrow had hatched a plan to visit the Monroes' archives. The only problem was, it hinged on the one person Sparrow could think of to drive her there—Auntie Geraldine.

Sparrow gritted her teeth and did what she had vowed never to do again—talk to her aunt.

When Sparrow entered the kitchen, Auntie Geraldine faced the stove and didn't turn around to say good morning even though she knew Auntie Geraldine heard her footsteps.

Sparrow felt these little moments were as important as the big ones, and Auntie Geraldine didn't do these well either. Unlike Auntie Geraldine, Mama had been good with the small stuff, greeting Sparrow each day with a smile and a kiss on top of her dark hair. She'd been good at the big stuff too, and Sparrow needed this kind of parent. Auntie Geraldine wasn't cut out for mothering, but from what she'd seen, Mason Casto was made to be a father. He showed kindness to Maeve and Johnny, greeting them with special handshakes and buying them Cokes, but he also wanted to make sure they grew up right. Like all good fathers, he tried to keep them from fighting and carrying on, and Sparrow looked forward to calling him her own.

Tomorrow was Saturday, the day of the Casto family party. *Her family party.* Her stomach did the little flip-floppy thing it always did when she thought about being Mason's daughter. She could hardly wait for the day to arrive, but the more she thought about it, the longer it seemed to take.

Auntie Geraldine sat down at the table with a cup of coffee.

"Are you going to Wesley Monroe's today?" Sparrow asked.

"Yes. He needs me to sign some papers." She wrapped her hands around the steaming mug even though the mercury in the thermometer outside the kitchen window touched ninety-five.

"Could I go with you today? Ansley invited me over." This was decidedly untrue.

"Ansley?"

Sparrow nodded enthusiastically.

"Are you sure you were invited?"

"I'm sure."

"If Ansley invited you, I suppose you can come along. I'd like to see you spending time with decent people for once. But don't touch anything over there. And don't be rude. And don't go dressed like that. Put on something nicer."

"Don't worry. I know how to behave." Sparrow shoved her chair back.

Auntie Geraldine gave Sparrow one of her famous glares. "I mean it, Sparrow."

"I will. Promise." She felt like sticking her tongue out, but controlled her impulse. She really needed to look at those archives, and if she got sassy with Auntie Geraldine, she'd lose her chance.

When Sparrow came downstairs dressed in her best pair of cutoff shorts and flip-flops, Auntie Geraldine sent her back upstairs to change again. She came down a second time in another pair of shorts. Sparrow didn't have many clothes. She only had two dresses, her funeral dress and her Easter dress. She was saving her Easter dress for the Casto family party, and she didn't expect to wear her funeral dress ever again.

"No," Auntie Geraldine said.

"I don't have anything else."

Auntie Geraldine sighed heavily and went upstairs. When she came back down, she had a shopping bag. "It's for your first day of school in Havisham. Don't ruin it."

Sparrow looked inside the bag. It held a blue-and-white dress. It looked like a sailor outfit. It was awful.

"I'll wait while you put it on."

"Maybe we should save it for my first day."

"I'm not taking you dressed like that. Put it on, or you're not going."

"Fine."

Sparrow went to her room and put on the horrible dress. She looked ridiculous. She stomped downstairs.

Auntie Geraldine waited for her at the bottom of the steps. She nodded once, hung her pocketbook on her arm, and strode out the door without saying a word to Sparrow.

Sparrow and Auntie Geraldine climbed into the gold Buick. Sparrow's legs stuck to the leather seats while her arms bristled with goose bumps from the cold air that blew from the air-conditioning. She reached for the vents to turn them away from her.

Auntie Geraldine swatted at her hand. "Don't touch those. I have them just as I like them."

"It's freezing in here."

"Don't be ridiculous. The temperature is set at sixty-eight degrees. It feels perfect."

Sparrow kicked off her shoes and pulled her knees into her chest for warmth even though she knew she wasn't supposed to put her feet on the seat. She was freezing.

Auntie Geraldine gave her a look but didn't say anything. She seemed to be playing nice today too. Sparrow wondered why.

When Auntie Geraldine finally turned the Buick onto the Monroes' drive, Sparrow leaned forward and craned her neck to see the trees from the window better. The Monroes' driveway ran at least a quarter of a mile long, and huge oak trees lined the entire way. They stretched high into the air and arched over the road, gracefully touching in the middle. Gray Spanish moss hung from the branches like necklaces. At the end of the drive, a plantation home sat at the water's edge.

Unlike Sparrow's water, the lawyer's water was part of the Intracoastal, a free-flowing waterway fit for boating and passage out to sea. It had none of the stagnant stillness or black, sucking silt of Sparrow's marsh.

Auntie Geraldine put the car in park, and Sparrow put her hand on the door handle. She thought about asking Auntie Geraldine why she hated Dalton House so much, why she hated Beulah, why she hated Sparrow, but Auntie Geraldine got out of the car before she had a chance. It was probably for the best. Auntie Geraldine wasn't someone Sparrow could talk to.

Sparrow got out of the car and followed Auntie Geraldine to the door.

Auntie Geraldine rang the Monroes' doorbell. She heard the gong echo inside the house and footsteps come toward the door. The massive front door opened and Sparrow found herself staring at another unfriendly face.

Ansley Monroe's.

CHAPTER TWENTY-THREE

Ansley Monroe stood in the doorway wearing a white tennis outfit and her blond hair in a ponytail. The Monroes were the only kids Sparrow knew who took lessons. Their mother drove them over to Havisham for tennis and piano.

Surprise flashed across Ansley's face, and then anger when she saw Sparrow standing next to Auntie Geraldine. Sparrow's allegiance with Maeve and Johnny had shifted her status from outsider to enemy in Ansley's eyes. Sparrow had spent her life being a neutral party, watching the skirmishes and the battles from the sidelines. Now she fought in the thick of the war. She hoped she had the skills to survive.

Auntie Geraldine shifted her pocketbook from one arm to the other. "Good morning, Ansley. I'm here to see your father and Sparrow has come along. She says you invited her over."

Ansley narrowed her eyes viciously at Sparrow.

Sparrow crossed her fingers behind her back and hoped Ansley would play nice in front of the grown-ups. It was a risky gamble.

"Sparrow—said—*I*—invited—*her*—over." Ansley repeated each word slowly as if trying to decode their meaning, which she probably was.

"She did." Auntie Geraldine seemed to be willing it to be true. Having Sparrow in with the Monroes elevated her status in a way that Auntie Geraldine respected.

Sparrow gave Ansley a look that she hoped said, *Play along, and you'll be glad you did.* "Remember at church when you said I should find friends other than the Castos?"

"At—church," Ansley repeated. She sounded like a robot. One more minute of this and Auntie Geraldine's suspicious nature would detect the ruse.

Luckily, the sound of heavy footsteps saved Sparrow. Mr. Monroe walked across the foyer to the door. "Ansley, who's at the door?"

Sparrow squeezed her crossed fingers tighter. She'd always thought of Mr. Monroe as a nice man. She hoped she was right.

He came up behind Ansley and put his hands on her shoulders. "Hello, Geraldine. And Sparrow. To what do we owe this honor?"

Sparrow answered before anyone else could. "Auntie Geraldine's come to see you, but Ansley invited me over to look at your archives. She said the next time my aunt visited I should come along. To look at your collection. She said it was fascinating."

Mr. Monroe beamed at his daughter. "Ansley, what a lovely invitation. I am quite proud of my collection, as Ansley well knows. I've been trying to get both children to take an interest for years. I'm thrilled it has finally taken root. We usually only show the archives by prearranged appointment, but since you have a personal invitation from Ansley, we'll make an exception."

Ansley looked like she wanted to skewer Sparrow, but she quickly fixed her expression before gazing up at her father. "You know I love anything you love, Daddy." She squeezed him around the waist.

Sparrow felt a combination of jealousy and annoyance. Ansley was lucky to have a parent who loved her, and Sparrow felt the aching pang that accompanied any reminder of what she lost when Mama died. On the other hand, it bothered her that Mr. Monroe seemed oblivious to Ansley's duplicity. Though she quickly checked herself. She had been employing a fair amount of trickery too.

"*Wonderful*," Auntie Geraldine said, a hint of suspicion

in her voice. Sparrow knew Auntie Geraldine wasn't completely fooled, but she appeared willing to overlook her misgivings. Auntie Geraldine would do anything to climb Beulah's social ladder. "Sounds like the perfect pastime for young ladies."

"I agree." Mr. Monroe practically glowed. "Let them in, sweetheart. Don't keep them standing on the front porch. We don't want to be rude." His tone held a warning note. Manners meant more than wealth in Beulah.

Without another word, Ansley stepped aside to let Auntie Geraldine and Sparrow in but rolled her eyes as Sparrow walked by her.

Sparrow stepped into a foyer so grand and sweeping she felt like an insect in a cave. Polished to a high sheen, the white marble floor looked as slick as still water, and the crystal chandelier shot rainbows of refracted light around the room. Sparrow caught Ansley watching her take in the hall, and she checked her reaction. She drew herself up and straightened her shoulders the way she'd seen Auntie Geraldine do when her pride got rankled.

"Geraldine, I suppose you're here about those papers. Follow me to my office and I'll get you started. Ansley and Sparrow, wait for me; I'll only be a moment."

"Sure," Ansley said.

Mr. Monroe cleared his throat.

Ansley quickly corrected herself. "Yes, sir."

As soon as Auntie Geraldine and Mr. Monroe were out of earshot, Ansley whirled on Sparrow. "Out with it. And it better be good."

It was, but telling Ansley the truth seemed like a very bad idea. It occurred to Sparrow that she hadn't expected to get this far, so hadn't planned for it. "Well . . . ," she said, stalling.

"I'm waiting." Ansley crossed her arms and tapped her foot. Even angry, Ansley looked perfect. Her white tennis dress and sneakers were so bright they practically sparkled. Even her shoelaces were white. "While you're at it, explain that dress."

Sparrow looked at her sailor dress. That was easier to explain. It really was awful. "My aunt bought it for me. She's a bit out of touch with what kids wear."

Ansley scoffed. "A bit? That's an understatement. Now out with the rest."

"I need to research a school project."

"No, you don't. We go to the same school, remember? And it's summer."

"It's a special project just for me."

"You're lying. This has something to do with those Castos, doesn't it?"

"No," Sparrow said as Mr. Monroe returned to the foyer.

"Daddy, she's been hanging out with those Castos. She's up to . . ." Ansley stopped. She seemed to remember that she had scored major points with her dad by pretending she had invited Sparrow over to look at his archives.

"You were saying, sweetheart?"

"Never mind, it's not important."

"Good. Why don't you get Sparrow some lemonade and meet us in the library."

"Anything for you, Daddy." Ansley smiled sweetly at her father and left for the kitchen. Her blond ponytail bounced cheerily as she walked away.

"The library is this way." Mr. Monroe started to place a kindly hand on Sparrow's shoulder and then withdrew as if he couldn't quite bring himself to touch her. He absently rubbed his fingers together as if removing microscopic grit he could feel but not see.

Sparrow pretended not to notice his withdrawal and repressed the sting of a rejection so infinitesimal and instinctual it felt fused to every thread that made up the fabric of Beulah. Sparrow's outcast status had not changed. It thrived. Like a root, it grew and snaked underground, hidden below layers of politeness.

Sparrow shoved the slight aside and followed him. At least she had Johnny and Maeve now. Elena too, she reminded herself.

As they walked, she did her best to take in the splendor. She had never been to a museum, but she imagined the experience would be similar to visiting the Monroes' family home. Gigantic oil paintings hung on the walls, pearly white statues decorated side tables, and knee-high vases overflowed with long-stem flowers. The place stunned her senses.

Their path took them by a room with French doors and floor-to-ceiling windows that overlooked the slow-flowing waters of the Intracoastal. A grand piano stood in the center of the room, and Andrew sat on its bench, gazing outside.

Mr. Monroe cleared his throat. Andrew immediately bent over the piano and started playing scales.

Sparrow thanked her lucky stars she didn't have lessons.

Mr. Monroe's library looked exactly the way a lawyer's library should. Shelves brimming with books lined the walls and a mahogany desk dominated one corner of the room. Sparrow wished Johnny was with her. He'd love it.

Mr. Monroe motioned for Sparrow to sit and then went to the bookshelves. "Are you interested in anything in particular? I have a record of the owners of your house going all the way back to the first Dalton who built it."

Sparrow already knew the builder had been Dewy Dalton, her great-great-great . . . Well, she didn't know how many greats he went back, but she did know he built the house and the swing she loved so much. "I'm particularly interested in Beulah folks from the year 1901."

"A historian on a mission, I see." He set a thick, newspaper-sized leather-bound book in front of Sparrow. "All the papers inside this book are from 1900 through 1905," Mr. Monroe explained.

She opened it and saw that it was actually full of newspapers. Five years of them. At the top of the yellowing pages, it read *Beulah Daily Herald*. "I didn't know Beulah use to have a daily paper." The *Herald* Sparrow read came out monthly and was typically only a few pages long.

He looked over her shoulder at the bound volume. "Oh, yes. At one time Beulah was up and coming, but when those folks up north rerouted the Cattail County–bound train through Havisham, the town's growth hit a snag. It never did recover."

"That's too bad," Sparrow said, flipping through the pages of the book, hoping something might catch her eye.

"Though I hope Beulah's fate will change when I purchase your property," Mr. Monroe said casually.

Sparrow's head shot up. "Did you say you're buying *my* house?"

"If we can get the details worked out. It's right off the main road, making it a great location for a strip mall."

She gaped at him. "A strip mall? What about the marsh?"

"That will have to be filled in, of course."

Sparrow's mind swarmed with images of bulldozers gobbling up marsh grasses while snowy egrets and skitter bugs fled for their lives. She also foresaw the slower destruction of the bigger predators who would be confronted by asphalt and speeding cars instead of their roaming lands. Sparrow's stomach rolled. She felt sick.

Every time she thought she was getting a leg up on Auntie Geraldine, some new betrayal surfaced. She had thought the idea of someone else living in Dalton House was the end of the world. Now she knew it wasn't. This was.

Sparrow pushed down the sick feeling so she could speak. "Get the details worked out? So you haven't bought it yet?"

"No. Not officially, yet. But soon."

It wasn't a done deal. Sparrow still had reason to hope. She forced herself to focus.

Tomorrow was the Casto family party. Maeve and Johnny had the proof she needed to claim Mason Casto as her father. Once she did, he would buy Dalton House. Johnny had vouched for Mason. He said Mason would do what needed to be done. Mason would save Dalton House, Sparrow would help the Boy, and the Boy would bring Mama back.

Sparrow prayed the gossip about Mason making a fortune in the oil business was true. If Mr. Monroe planned to build a strip mall, he must be offering Auntie Geraldine a lot of money for the property. They were going to need a fortune to wrangle Dalton House from the Monroes' clutches.

Ansley walked into the library. She held a glass of lemonade in one hand and a cloth napkin in the other.

"Ansley, that's lovely. Your timing is perfect," Mr. Monroe said as he turned back to the bookshelves.

Ansley handed the lemonade and the napkin to Sparrow.

Sparrow found her polite voice and said, "Thank you."

"My pleasure, I'm sure," Ansley answered, just as pleasantly.

Sparrow took a sip of lemonade and nearly spat it out all over the newspapers. Ansley had filled the glass with salt instead of sugar.

Ansley smirked. "Enjoying the archives?"

Sparrow took another sip of lemonade to prove she could. She had no intention of letting the Monroes best her. She set the glass on top of the cloth napkin. "Thank you, Ansley. This is delicious."

Ansley huffed and plopped down in a chair.

Mr. Monroe turned around with another big book. He'd been so caught up in his search for tidbits of Beulah history to share with Sparrow he'd missed the entire exchange between the girls. Sparrow begrudgingly gave Ansley credit. She knew how to be sneaky, that was for sure. Sparrow would find it nearly impossible to pull off a prank like that right under Auntie Geraldine's nose.

"The record of your family tree is in here." Mr. Monroe placed a new book on top of the other one. He thumbed through it until he found a page entitled THE DALTON FAMILY.

Sparrow moved the lemonade glass as far away from her as possible. She examined her family tree. She traced the lines going up and out. She found Mama's name and then Auntie Geraldine's. Two sprouts from the same branch, though they were nothing alike. She followed the branches to where her name should be recorded, but there was no entry.

Mr. Monroe leaned over Sparrow's shoulder. "Hmm . . . we seem to be out of date. We'll have to get that fixed."

Sparrow wondered if he would. She shut the book and pulled the bound newspapers to her. She flipped page after page, scanning headlines. She felt like she was looking for a needle in a haystack. Then she saw "Orphan Train Rider Adopted." The word *orphan* stopped her. The way she kept running into it, she felt like it was taunting her.

Mr. Monroe leaned over her shoulder. "Yes, that's an interesting story. As you know, we're quite proud of our family's commitment to philanthropic causes, and it all started with that orphan train."

The phrase *orphan train* pecked at Sparrow's brain like a rooster looking for scratch. It made her edgy, like nothing good could come of those two words together. "What's an orphan train?"

"Ansley, get one of our books for Sparrow, would you?"

"Is she going to pay for it? The proceeds are for charity," Ansley said haughtily.

His smile tightened. "Oh, I think we can afford to spare one copy for a fellow historian."

Ansley rolled her eyes but left obediently.

Mr. Monroe watched his daughter go and then turned back to Sparrow. "In the nineteen hundreds, there were so many orphans roaming the streets of New York that a minister came up with a grand idea. He decided to put the children on trains and send them across the United States to find new families. Mostly, the trains went to western states, but my ancestors arranged for a train to be sent to Cattail County."

Sparrow quickly read the article. At a New York City depot, thirty orphans had been put on a train headed to Cattail County. As the train made its way down the coast, it made several stops. At each depot along the way, the children were lined up on the platform and offered up for adoption. By the time the train reached Beulah, there was only one child left—a boy. The Monroe family took him home. The fact that the Monroes not only organized the train but also took a child in was looked on as a great charity, and the Monroes were praised for their altruistic deeds.

"It's because of my ancestors' involvement in organizing that train I wrote the book." Pride filled Mr. Monroe's voice and he seemed to stand taller.

Ansley walked in carrying a thin paperback. "Here you go, Daddy."

Mr. Monroe took the book from Ansley. He got a fancy pen from his desk and signed the inside cover with a flourish. He handed the book to Sparrow. "For you."

Sparrow stared at the title. *Orphan Trains: Small Towns, Big Hearts.* Knowing that a train full of parentless children had sped down the railway to Cattail County in search of families made Sparrow's throat tighten. She didn't like living with Auntie Geraldine, but at least she had a place to call home . . . for now.

"Unfortunately, that foray into philanthropy ended badly."

"What happened?"

"Don't tell that part of the story, Daddy," Ansley said. "It ruins the first part."

"It's a sad story, dear, but no fault of ours. One can only offer a helping hand. Whether or not the offer is accepted is up to the recipient." Mr. Monroe quickly flipped through the pages until he found another article. It read "Orphan Thief Dies." He tapped the page.

"The orphan was a *thief*?" Sparrow felt it was awfully unfair to label a kid as both an orphan and a thief.

Mr. Monroe shrugged. "A lot of those street children were pickpockets and ruffians. Habits are hard to break. As the story goes, the boy became obsessed with a Monroe family heirloom. The orphan insisted the heirloom was his. He claimed his father had given it to him before he died. A ridiculous claim, of course. Imagine a penniless orphan with an heirloom?"

"What was the heirloom?" Sparrow asked, transfixed by the story.

"Sadly, specific details have been lost over time, but some versions of the story mention a timepiece. What I do know is one night the orphan stole the heirloom and ran away, causing his own death. My family never did get it back. No good deed goes unpunished, I guess."

Dread settled into the pit of Sparrow's stomach and spread out like a weed, invading her whole body, and though she feared the answer, she asked the question. "How did he die?"

"After he ran away, they called out the hounds, of course. The dogs easily picked up his scent. He was a city kid, you understand, not accustomed to our marshlands, but he got surprisingly far. When he heard the dogs coming for him, he ran into the swamp. Unfortunately, the night he ran away there was a king tide. I'm sure you can imagine what happened. You know the warnings."

"He drowned in the marsh?"

"Yes. Out by your place, actually. Where we'll be building the strip mall. Who knows? Once we start to dig, maybe we'll find that lost family heirloom." Mr. Monroe rubbed his elegant fingers together expectantly, as if he already held his missing heirloom between them.

The revelation slammed into Sparrow—the orphan had died in her marsh. She felt the blood drain from her face.

The Monroes' orphan was her Boy, and his story squeezed her heart tighter than a vise.

Mr. Monroe scrutinized Sparrow. "Are you sure you're well? You look like you've seen a ghost."

Sparrow hadn't seen a ghost. She'd found one.

CHAPTER TWENTY-FOUR

Sparrow and Auntie Geraldine didn't speak to each other on the way home from the Monroes'.

Auntie Geraldine stared straight ahead, navigating the back roads with the precision of a local, while Sparrow stole sideways glances at her in search of signs of her traitorous nature. Sparrow thought of all the times Auntie Geraldine questioned Sparrow's claim to the Dalton name. Auntie Geraldine had some nerve. No rightful Dalton would EVER consider selling the house and the marsh, much less to the Monroes so they could build a strip mall. Every time she pictured the Monroes' bulldozers digging up the marsh, Sparrow's stomach rolled.

Sparrow stared out the window and let her mind drift toward the Boy. At the thought of him, her throat constricted and a weight settled on her heart.

Her new knowledge of the Boy's last hours tormented her. She couldn't stop envisioning the rising tide or the all-encompassing darkness of the marsh at night. Even with a full moon, shadows shifted and morphed into strange shapes that hammered at the nerves and unsettled the mind. The marsh at night was no place for a kid and a horrible place to die.

Sparrow thought about the way Mr. Monroe had spoken about the Boy. He had called him a pickpocket and a ruffian, but the description didn't fit.

The Boy was mischievous sometimes, but never malicious. He was most likely to act up when Sparrow needed a friend. When he blew the dirt at Mama's funeral, Sparrow had not wanted anyone to throw dirt onto her casket. When he hit Auntie Geraldine in the shin with the swing, Sparrow had wanted to be left alone and not forced to talk to people. When he slammed the screen door, Auntie Geraldine had been yelling at Sparrow. That day with Ansley and Andrew, they had ganged up on her and called her an orphan.

And when no one else was there for her after Mama died, the Boy had been her only comfort. Her only friend.

Sparrow bit her lip. Mr. Monroe's accusation didn't make sense. Sparrow knew in her heart the Boy wasn't a thief. He was a good soul. She wasn't sure how, but Mr. Monroe had gotten his story terribly wrong.

When Auntie Geraldine pulled into the drive, Sparrow pushed open the car door and hopped out before Auntie

Geraldine had a chance to put the car in park. She stormed up the front steps and let the screen door slam shut.

Auntie Geraldine sniped at Sparrow, but Sparrow wasn't listening.

There had never been a Dalton more awful than Auntie Geraldine. There had never been anyone more awful than her, period.

Sparrow went to her bedroom and locked the door. She changed out of the horrible sailor dress and threw it in the corner. She'd never wear that ghastly thing again.

Sparrow sat on her window seat and unfolded the newspaper articles.

Mr. Monroe had kindly made copies of the first article for her when she asked, thrilled that she'd taken an interest in the story of the orphan train. Especially since it pertained to a part of his heritage that made him proud to be a Monroe.

He had been less thrilled when she'd asked for a copy of the second article, the one that detailed the Boy's death, but had complied anyway. Beulah's strict adherence to manners allowed Sparrow to get her way.

The second article told the Boy's story just as Mr. Monroe had. He had become obsessed with a family heirloom and run away. But what Mr. Monroe hadn't told her was the Boy had hidden at Dalton House. The Boy had made it all the way out to her house and had sought refuge on the front porch.

Sparrow read the relevant part of the article. *When the orphan thief heard the hounds approach, he burst through the screen door of the Dalton place. He ran into the marsh in an attempt to throw the dogs off his scent. Acutely aware of the many dangers of the swamp, the sheriff's men wisely gave up the chase at the shore. They waited on the bank and called to the orphan thief, but he refused to heed their warnings.*

Sparrow recalled her nighttime experience in the marsh. At the mere thought of that night, primal fear shot through her, and her body tingled as if electrified. The marsh had truly frightened her and she was a local. For a city kid like the Boy, it must have been terrifying. Sparrow's heart wrenched.

She took a deep breath to brace herself for what would come next and scanned the rest of the newspaper article. The night the Boy ran away, the moon had been full. Shortly after the Boy went into the marsh, a huge storm rolled in, and it started to rain. Then the tide started to rise.

The Boy never came out of the marsh again. He had walked into the marsh on a full moon at high tide. He never had a chance.

Tears rolled down Sparrow's cheeks. The Boy's death had been tragic and lonely. As much as she loved the marsh, it had a dark side. The wild landscape sometimes claimed what didn't belong. She swiped her cheeks and vowed to help the Boy find peace.

Sparrow set aside the article and opened the book Mr. Monroe had given her, *Orphan Trains: Small Towns, Big Hearts*. The book chronicled the train's journey from New York City to Beulah. It talked about each town the train stopped at on the way south and gave a history of all the families who adopted kids.

There was very little mention of the orphans themselves, which Sparrow found rather neglectful and sad. She felt like no one cared about the kids who got adopted.

Sparrow flipped to the back of the book and discovered a collection of photographs. There were a lot of pictures of the Monroes' ancestors, and on the very last page was a picture of the all the orphan train riders before they left New York City.

A black-and-white photo showed thirty children of all ages lined up in a row. There were even a couple of babies being held by older kids.

Looking at all those parentless kids pulled at Sparrow. Even though they had lived their lives long before she had been born, she knew exactly how each one of them felt at the moment that photograph had been taken—heartsick.

Sparrow looked at each face one by one; she wanted to honor them by truly seeing them. When she got to the middle of the first row, recognition made her heart flap against her chest like a butterfly trying to escape a jar.

In the center of the front row a boy with round cherub cheeks and dark hair cut close posed with a cocky stance. He wore a white dress shirt unbuttoned at the neck and cuffs, black pants a tad too short, and black boots unlaced with the tongues flapping. Her Boy.

She carefully tore the picture out of the book and drew the page close.

Sparrow's body went numb. Dangling from his hand was her pocket watch.

Sparrow's mind raced to process the facts. Mr. Monroe had mentioned a timepiece, and Sparrow wondered if the Boy's pocket watch and the missing family heirloom were one and the same. They had to be . . . but if the Boy had the watch before he got on the train in New York, then Mr. Monroe was wrong about him. He'd not been a ruffian and a thief. He had not stolen a family heirloom from the Monroes. He'd reclaimed what belonged to him in the first place.

And if the Boy was innocent, then Sparrow had found it. The thing the Boy needed for peace—her pocket watch.

CHAPTER TWENTY-FIVE

On Saturday morning, Sparrow awoke with a renewed sense of hope. If all went as planned, by the end of the day, she would have everything her heart desired—the Boy, Mama, Dalton House, and a daddy.

Eli had been right. The Monroes' archives were the key to discovering the Boy's story. She now knew what he needed to give him peace—the pocket watch. She remembered the Boy's face the day she had taken it to sell to the watch vendor. He had reached out and tried to grab it, but she had closed her fingers over it, keeping it from him. Every time she remembered that moment, her throat got tight.

But now that she knew, she could fix everything. She'd return the watch to the Boy, and the Boy would help Mama. Eli told Sparrow he would have the watch for her on Saturday. That was today, the same day as the Casto family party. She'd go get it right after. Maeve and Johnny could go with her.

Now that the day of the Casto family party had arrived,

Sparrow's emotions twisted and tangled into a confusing array of contradictions. Excitement, nervousness, and a touch of sadness coiled in her belly like a slipknot. She wondered if she could be two things at once—a Dalton and a Casto.

Sparrow pulled her Easter dress out of the closet. The day Mama bought it for Sparrow had been one of the last times they'd gone out together. Mama drove Sparrow to Havisham to shop at the children's clothing store there. Mama watched as Sparrow tried on dress after dress until they'd finally settled on a lilac one with a matching hat and gloves. They'd bought black patent-leather shoes, and a purse to go with it, an unexpected extravagance. Then they had a fancy lunch at a nice restaurant. Sparrow wished Mama had shared all her secrets that day because they ran out of time after that. Mama started resting a lot, and Auntie Geraldine moved into Dalton House to take care of her, which she seemed to think meant keeping Sparrow out of the way.

Holding on to Mama felt like carrying water in her palms; every second a bit more of her slipped away and she wanted to keep as much as she could.

Sparrow tucked Mama's picture, the newspaper articles, and the picture from Mr. Monroe's book in her purse and slid it on her arm. Then she put on her sneakers. She was walking to the Castos', and she couldn't do that in fancy shoes, so she decided not to wear them. By the end of the day, she'd be part Casto anyway, and shoes would be optional.

Sparrow climbed out her window and down her oak.

The walk to the Castos' was a long one. Finally, the Casto place came into view.

The run-down house leaned precariously atop one-story stilts that raised the building off the ground so that air flowed under it. In theory, the elevation kept the house cool. In truth, nothing could combat the Beulah heat.

Rusty bikes and half-broken toys littered the front lawn, and a rope sagged low, heavy with clothes. At the far end of the property, a dingy white trailer was parked under the oak trees. This was a new addition to the Casto land, and was Mason's home. In comparison, Dalton House was a mansion.

Sparrow knocked on the front door. She heard a TV blaring and lots of people talking, but no one answered.

She knocked harder.

When nobody came, she hammered on the door with her fist.

Finally, she heard footsteps and then the door opened. Clara Casto answered the door.

Clara looked Sparrow up and down. "You look right nice. Is that your Easter dress?" Everyone in Beulah went to church on Easter Sunday dressed in their finest.

"Yep, I'm here for the party."

Clara turned to look at the clock on the wall. "You're a bit early, but I expect Maeve and Johnny will be happy to see you just the same. They've been trying to find a way to get out of chores all morning. How did it go with the fortune-teller?"

"Good. How about you? Are you going to Vanderbilt?" Sparrow asked.

"The fortune-teller was pretty vague, but I decided my chances are good. I've got the grades, so I'm putting my faith in that. I'll get Maeve and Johnny for you." She turned and called, "Maeve! Johnny! Someone here to see y'all!"

"Who is it?" Maeve asked suspiciously from somewhere near the back of the house. "It better not be any Monroes."

Clara rolled her eyes. "Maeve, come to the door. It's Sparrow Dalton here for the party."

Maeve ran to the front door. "Why didn't you say so?" She grabbed Sparrow by the arm and ran into the yard, tugging Sparrow behind her. "Come on. Johnny's back here."

Sparrow laughed as Maeve sprinted around the house, pulling Sparrow along. When they got to a small shed, Maeve burst through the door.

"Look who's here!"

Inside the shed, Johnny sat on an old lawn chair pulled close to the back wall. A large space between the boards let the light through, and Johnny was using beams of sunlight to read by. Johnny looked up. He stuck a bookmark into what looked near to the end of a huge book and stood up. "Great! You're early."

Sparrow surveyed the book Johnny put down, taking in the hundreds upon hundreds of tissue-thin pages, and a deep respect for his reading ability emerged. He was way smarter than anyone knew. The book had to be five hundred pages at least. Sparrow hadn't cracked a book all summer, and here he sat reading that tome on a Saturday afternoon.

"You look great, Sparrow," Johnny said. "Is that your Easter dress?"

Sparrow's cheeks got hot. "I think I might have over-dressed. Y'all are wearing your normal clothes."

"We'll fancy up in a bit, but forget that for now. We've got something to give you." Maeve danced around delightedly.

Sparrow's heart skipped a happy beat. "Okay, but I have to show you something first. I got into the Monroes' archives."

"*Archives.*" Maeve looked disappointed until Sparrow pulled out the newspaper articles and started to read. Then she showed them the Boy's picture from *Orphan Trains: Small Towns, Big Hearts.*

"That's *him?*" Maeve said. "He doesn't look creepy at all." She sounded disappointed.

"I told you he was a kid like us."

Johnny whistled. "So, that orphan train rider is your ghost? He looks like a nice fellow."

"He is. But that's not even the best part. I know what he wants." Sparrow told them about the watch and pointed to it in the picture. "That's the same watch Eli took to research."

"That's great news!" Maeve said.

"Eli said he'd have my watch back today. After the party, let's go to the flea market. We can pick it up and tell Elena what I discovered."

"It's a plan," Maeve said.

"Now we have something to show you." Johnny got up and went over to a bin filled with old rags. He dug down to the bottom and pulled out a manila envelope, stuffed full. "This is for you."

"What is it?" Sparrow asked, feeling the weight of the packet.

Johnny smiled proudly like he'd just discovered the secrets of the universe. "Your custody papers."

"What's that?" Sparrow asked.

"Legal papers that say who gets to raise you. We found them in our uncle's trailer."

"Does this mean what I think it means?"

"Yep. That's the proof you need," Maeve said.

"Are you sure?" Sparrow stroked the thick packet.

"Absolutely, positively," Johnny said. "We've been keeping tabs on Uncle—"

Maeve interrupted. "We've been following him, actually."

"Anyway, he keeps going over to Wesley Monroe's and your aunt is going over there all the time too."

"They've been fighting about you, deciding who's goin' to get you. And Uncle Mason's finally won," Johnny said.

Sparrow felt certain Auntie Geraldine wasn't fighting for her, but she liked the part about Mason winning.

"Johnny wants to be a lawyer when he grows up, so he knows a lot about this kind of thing," Maeve said. "He's been reading up on it since we found that photo of your mama."

Sparrow looked over at the book. *Florida Family Law* was etched into the spine with gold lettering. She counted her lucky stars to have Maeve and Johnny on her side. "Did you open this?" Sparrow asked.

"No, we thought you should be the first. He's your daddy, after all," Johnny said gently.

"And now you're officially our cousin." Maeve put her arm around Sparrow. "Which means we're pretty much Daltons. I can't wait for those stuck-up Monroes to find out. Everything's falling into place perfectly."

"I know." By the end of the day, Sparrow would have Mason, Mama, the Boy, and Dalton House.

Maeve grinned and squeezed Sparrow's shoulder. "Aren't you excited?"

Sparrow was so excited her soul felt like dancing. She hugged the envelope tight and twirled.

Maeve laughed and Sparrow's heart rode that happy sound like a wave. This was going to be the best day of her life.

CHAPTER TWENTY-SIX

In the end, Sparrow decided she wanted to open the papers with Mason. She felt it would be more memorable that way. She imagined the two of them sitting down after the Casto family party to read the official documents together. He'd smile proudly, knowing she was his daughter, and Sparrow would be so happy to finally have a father.

She put the packet back under the pile of rags and followed Maeve and Johnny to the house so they could put on their party clothes.

Sparrow waited for them in the Casto living room. At first, she struggled to find a place to sit. Grown-ups bustled around the kitchen, making food, while a bunch of little Castos sat in front of the television watching a show turned up way too loud. She finally spied a spot on the couch between two baby Castos sharing a box of Cheerios. Sparrow sat down and put the box on her lap. The baby Castos didn't seem to mind. They just kept digging into the box, grabbing huge handfuls of cereal that barely made it into their mouths.

The whole room burst with Casto cousins, but Sparrow didn't know who belonged to who. Now that she belonged to this huge clan, Maeve and Johnny needed to tutor her on the family tree.

After a while, Maeve came into the living room. She looked nicer than normal, wearing a shorts romper in a floral pattern, but Sparrow had definitely overdressed.

One of the baby Castos threw a Cheerio at Maeve and she stuck her tongue out at him.

In response, both babies stuck their tongues out at Maeve. Sparrow watched the exchange with fascination. She had a lot to learn about being part of a large family.

Maeve pulled Sparrow off the couch. "Let's get the good food before it's all gone."

"What about Johnny?"

"He's coming." Maeve walked outside and Sparrow followed her.

Somehow, the Castos had managed to transform the yard in the time it'd taken Maeve to change her clothes. All the toys had been put away and a long table had been set up. It held platters upon platters of food. Buckets filled with ice and drinks sat next to the table.

Everywhere Sparrow looked, there were redheaded Castos—young ones, old ones, and every age in between ones. The little ones ran around, while the oldest Castos sat in folding chairs in the shade. Many of the guests were already eating.

"Darn it," Maeve said. "They've already started. Load up now. If you wait, there'll be nothing left. This family is like a plague of locusts." Maeve grabbed a paper plate and filled it so high with food, Sparrow marveled that it didn't topple off onto the ground.

Sparrow followed Maeve's lead, taking a plate and some food, but she didn't take as much as Maeve. Her stomach was too full of butterflies to have space for food.

The girls found a spot of shade and sat in the grass. Maeve dug into her food while Sparrow watched her new family with interest. She tried to figure out their number by counting them, but the Castos wouldn't cooperate. They kept moving from place to place. Sparrow was in the middle of her second attempt at a head count when she spied Wesley Monroe and the twins.

She nudged Maeve in the ribs to get her attention. "Look over there."

Maeve was partway through a second ear of corn. She looked up, saw the Monroes, and groaned. "Ignore them."

Sparrow thought that was good advice. She was still annoyed about the lemonade.

Johnny found them and sat down. He had a plate piled high with food. "I love family parties."

The three kids sat on the grass eating and talking about nothing and everything at the same time, and Sparrow felt she could spend the rest of her life there with them. Being with Maeve and Johnny didn't make Sparrow miss Mama less, though it did feel more bearable, like the relief of an unexpected lending hand when lugging a heavy load.

Music started to play and they moved closer to the band. A pack of scruffy, redheaded Castos strummed and plucked a hodgepodge collection of instruments. Fiddles, banjos, guitars, and even a washboard responded melodiously to their deft fingers. Sparrow tapped her foot and clapped her hands along with everyone else as warmth filled her belly. She loved everything about her new family.

When the band paused briefly between songs to tune their instruments, Sparrow heard a sarcastic snort behind her. "It's like a hillbilly fest out here."

All three kids turned.

Ansley Monroe stood behind them, sneering.

Maeve's broad smile fell away and her hands turned into fists.

Johnny put a hand on his sister's arm. "Remember what Uncle Mason said?"

"I think they're really good," Sparrow offered, trying to dispel the tension.

"What are you even doing here, swamp rat?"

"She's our friend," Maeve said.

Ansley snorted. "The weird just get weirder."

Maeve's face flushed and her eyes flashed with anger. "Don't you dare talk about her like that. She's not just our friend. She's family."

"Maeve," Johnny said. "Don't. It isn't your news."

"It's okay," Sparrow said.

"What are y'all going on about?" Ansley asked.

Sparrow felt nerves and other things twist in her stomach. She wasn't sure she was ready to say it out loud yet, but if she was going to be a Casto, she had to be loyal like one. Maeve and Johnny had thrown their lot in with her and now it was her turn. "Mason Casto's my father."

At first, Ansley laughed. "You're joking."

United, Sparrow, Maeve, and Johnny held their ground, faces stern, arms crossed.

"Prove it," Ansley said.

Andrew joined them. "What's going on over here?"

Ansley smirked. "Sparrow Dalton thinks she's a Casto."

"Huh?"

"She says Mason Casto's her father and now she's going to prove it. Aren't you, Sparrow?"

Sparrow hated the way Ansley taunted her and she intended to wipe that smirk right off Ansley's face. "Johnny, do you mind getting those papers?"

"Do you think that's a good idea?"

"Yes."

"Are you sure?"

Sparrow nodded. "A hundred percent."

Johnny dashed off. In a flash, he came back with the envelope. He really did run fast. He handed the papers to Sparrow.

Sparrow showed them to Ansley and Andrew. "These are my custody papers. Your own daddy wrote them. That's why Mason's been at your house so much this summer."

Ansley's eyes narrowed as a smile played at her lips.

Andrew looked confused. "They've been . . ."

Ansley stopped her brother in midsentence. "Does Mason Casto know you have those?"

"Not yet. We're talking after the party," Sparrow said.

"I'll believe you, if you tell him now," Ansley countered, forcing Sparrow's hand. Ansley sought her revenge for the baseball game, Long's, and the archives, but Sparrow held all the cards. Ansley was going to lose.

"Sparrow," Johnny said. "It's okay. You don't need to prove anything to them."

Sparrow looked at Maeve. It might be all right for Johnny, but it wouldn't be okay for Maeve. Maeve had done so much for Sparrow and it was Sparrow's turn to prove her loyalty.

"What do I have to lose?" she asked, smiling. "The proof is right here." She hugged the papers confidently.

Sparrow stepped away from the kids and searched the crowd for Mason. She spotted him standing in a small crowd of folks. He slapped another Casto on the back and then laughed. He seemed really happy. She walked over to him, clutching the thick envelope like a treasure.

She cleared her throat. "Mason?"

He didn't hear her, so she put her hand on his arm and said again, "Mason?"

He turned. All of a sudden he seemed to be standing in a huge crowd rather than a small one and everyone watched as he said, "Having a good time, Sparrow?"

"Yes, great . . . um." Sparrow looked over at Maeve and Johnny standing next to a laughing Ansley, and her resolve strengthened. "I know," she said.

Mason cocked his head to the side. "Know what?"

"About this," she said, pointing to the papers.

Mason took the papers from her. "Where'd you find these?"

"It doesn't matter. What's important is that I know."

"I planned to tell everyone today. That's what this party is for."

Sparrow beamed. "I was going to talk to you today too. To let you know . . ." Sparrow paused, savoring the moment, and then continued, "I know you're my father."

232

Mason's eyes grew wide.

A Casto standing near Mason whistled in surprise and the group turned away to give them privacy. Though they didn't go too far. Instead, they lingered within earshot to make sure they heard everything being said.

Mason's forehead furrowed. "What do you think these papers are?"

"My custody papers."

Mason ran his hand through his hair. He seemed upset.

Sparrow bit her lip. This wasn't the reaction she'd hoped for. She'd expected to be swept up in a fatherly hug or treated to a special handshake at least. She'd never expected to see shock and worry overwhelm Mason's kind features.

"Sparrow, I'm really sorry. These aren't custody papers. These are ownership papers. They say I own the 76 station."

"Then do you have the other ones? The ones you've been working on with Wesley Monroe and Auntie Geraldine?"

Mason gently pulled Sparrow farther away from the crowd. "I've not been there with your aunt, Sparrow. She just happened to be there too sometimes. Where'd you get all this information?"

Sparrow looked over at Maeve and Johnny.

Maeve smiled and gave her the thumbs-up sign.

Johnny looked worried.

Ansley hugged her side. She shook so hard with laughter that she'd doubled over to keep from falling on the ground. And just like that, Sparrow knew. She was no one's daughter.

CHAPTER TWENTY-SEVEN

Shame and embarrassment washed over Sparrow like a tidal wave, and she did the only thing she could think of—run. She ran away from the Castos as far and as fast as she could. She thought she heard Maeve and Johnny calling her name, but she kept going. Maeve had befriended Sparrow because she believed Sparrow was a Casto and because Maeve wanted to be related to a Dalton. Now that it had proved false, so had their friendship.

No, there wasn't anything for her at the Castos, and she was too humiliated to look back anyway. Too many people heard her claim Mason Casto was her father, and news of her disgrace would spread like wildfire. By nightfall, all of Beulah would know.

She ran until she reached the old country road and her legs and lungs finally betrayed her. Reluctantly, she slowed to a walk. Her slower pace let her mind race and she struggled to keep her thoughts from tumbling over each other like waves.

She heard the rumble of a truck coming up the road behind her, and she moved to the shoulder to give it plenty of room to pass. Instead of driving by, it drove up beside her and slowed.

Mason Casto rolled down his window. "Mind if we talk for a sec?"

Maeve and Johnny were in the back, but neither said anything, and Sparrow avoided looking at them. The sight of them reminded her of everything she'd almost had.

Sparrow shrugged.

Mason pulled over and got out of his truck. They were near the little roadside cemetery, and he walked in that direction. He went through the gate and sat on a stone bench under an oak tree.

Sparrow joined him.

"You left this," Mason said. He cradled her small black purse in his large hands.

"Thanks." Sparrow took her bag, grateful to have it back. Inside was her picture of Mama and the information about the Boy.

"I'm sorry about Maeve and Johnny. They mean well. They're just a bit misguided sometimes."

"It's not their fault. We all thought it," Sparrow said. She opened her purse and gave Mason the photograph of Mama. She leaned against an old pickup truck at the flea market, and the words *Love never says goodbye* were inscribed on the back. "You had this."

Mason took the photo. He smiled. "Yes."

"You loved her," Sparrow said. "Johnny told me you fell in love at the flea market while looking through a bin of old gospel records."

Mason nodded. "I did love her. With all my heart, and it's true I fell in love with her that night. But she loved someone else."

"Who?" Sparrow asked.

"I don't know. She never told me. Did you know she'd gone away to college?"

Sparrow nodded. She had a vague memory of Mama mentioning it, but she didn't know any details about her time at college. There was so much Sparrow didn't know about Mama and so many things they never got to talk about. That was one of the hardest things about Mama being gone. All of her chances to know Mama and for Mama to know Sparrow stopped the day she died.

"She did. She was so smart. She was always real good in school. She got a scholarship and everything. Anyway, she'd come home that first summer bursting with new ideas and in love with someone else. This photo of her was for someone else. The writing on the back was for someone else. She dropped it, and I picked it up. I should have given it back to her. But knowing she was in love with someone else . . . Lordy, it ached." Mason clasped his hands in front of him and stared at the horizon as if the past were being reenacted there.

Sparrow waited for him to continue.

"That fall, she left again, and by the time she came back for Christmas, I was gone. I couldn't stay here without her. Everything reminded me of her. The clouds, the grass, the rain . . . love's a powerful thing."

Sparrow swallowed the lump in her throat. "That's how I feel." The words struggled out, barely a whisper.

"I know," Mason said. "It will get better."

"How?"

"Time is the only thing. You'll never forget her, but sometime, sooner than you think, it won't hurt so much to think on her. The memories will be good."

A breeze made the oak leaves overhead shiver and sunlight dappled Mason's face.

"I thought you were trying to get custody of me," Sparrow said, circling back to their earlier conversation.

"I know. Johnny, the lawyer. Those two." Mason shook his head.

At the thought of Johnny and Maeve, a fresh wave of heartache washed over Sparrow. She'd not only lost a father; she'd lost a whole family. Since her allegiance with Maeve and Johnny, Sparrow had not felt so alone. Now she was back where she'd started, the last Dalton offspring with Auntie Geraldine her only living relative. Sparrow really was an orphan.

"Should we give you a lift home?"

"No." Sparrow shook her head. "I'll walk."

Mason patted Sparrow on the knee, and Sparrow saw the contrast of his skin against hers. His skin was the ruddy, sun-baked color of bricks while hers was the same tawny shade she wore year-round. The shade of her skin didn't depend on the season, like Mason's. No. He wasn't her father, and deep down she'd known that all along.

"I wish I was your dad, Sparrow. You're a great kid."

Sparrow nodded. Wishing he was her dad wasn't the same thing as him being her dad.

CHAPTER TWENTY-EIGHT

Sparrow did not go home. Instead, she went to get the Boy's watch.

She'd lost an entire family and her hope of saving Dalton House in the course of an afternoon, and the only thing keeping her going was knowing that when she returned the watch to the Boy, he would bring Mama back as he promised.

At the thought of Mama, Sparrow's heart twisted. She would have never gone looking for a daddy over at the Castos if Mama had been by her side. Navigating the world without Mama was like being cast adrift without a compass. Mama's love for Sparrow was her true north, the magnetic pull that kept her on course. Without it, Sparrow didn't know how to find her way.

When Sparrow got to the flea market, she noticed the quiet emptiness of the field. A few tourists poked through half-packed boxes, but the hustle and bustle of previous days had died. The flea market was winding down for the year.

Sparrow found Elena's periwinkle van and knocked softly on the door.

"Who is it?" Elena asked in her curt, un-Beulah-like manner.

"It's me."

Elena slid the door open, and when she saw Sparrow, her brow creased. "Everything okay?"

Sparrow knew her red, swollen eyes told their own tale. "It's a long story."

Elena moved aside so Sparrow could climb into the van and then peeked out the door. "Are Maeve and Johnny with you?"

Sparrow flinched. The mention of Maeve and Johnny stung like salt on a wound. "No."

"Are they hiding somewhere?" Elena looked around the field dramatically, trying to cheer Sparrow.

"Not this time," Sparrow said, answering Elena's light-hearted comment without humor.

Elena's smile faded, and worry softened her voice. "That bad, huh? Do you want to tell me what's going on?"

Sparrow longed to tell Elena all about the party. It would be a relief to share how she felt with her friend, but shame and sadness constricted her throat, making it hard to speak.

"I came to pick up my watch from Eli and to tell you what I found at the archives."

"Tell me everything." Elena pulled Sparrow over to the little table to sit down. She pushed aside a suitcase that lay open on the bench. Elena had been packing.

"You're leaving?"

"We are. The flea market is winding down, and it's time to head back to New York." Elena's impending departure felt like another blow. Sparrow didn't know if she had the strength to keep losing people she cared about.

"What about your trip? Following in your grandmother's footsteps?"

Elena smiled. "Beulah was the last stop. And I'm ready to go home. It's weird, but hanging out in Beulah with you guys has made me feel . . ." Elena shrugged. "Don't laugh, but like it's okay to be me. It won't be so hard at school next year knowing I have three friends down here who like the tarot card me and the regular me. Who knows, maybe next summer, Eli will bring me back."

Sparrow knew exactly what Elena meant. Maeve and Johnny had made her feel that way too.

"Anyway, tell me how you got into the archives."

Sparrow told Elena about making Auntie Geraldine take her to the Monroes' and tricking Ansley into saying she'd invited her over. When Sparrow told Elena about the lemonade, she laughed at just the right place.

"So, what did you find out?"

Sparrow handed Elena the newspaper article about the Monroes adopting the Boy. "You thought to ask for a copy? That was smart. Eli does that."

Sparrow shrugged. "I'm glad I did. I didn't have a chance to read both articles all the way through at the Monroes'. When I got home, I found out something really important in the second one."

Elena bit her lip as she read the first article. When she finished, she looked up and said, "Those poor kids. It must have been terrible for them to be shipped off to strangers. I wish I knew how they ended up. I hope they found good homes."

"Me too." Sparrow thought about the other kids on the train. She hoped, unlike the Boy, their stories had happy endings.

"Do you think the orphan adopted by the Beulah family is your ghost?" Elena asked, pulling Sparrow from her reverie.

"I know it's him." Sparrow showed Elena the second article. "Mr. Monroe told me that the orphan died in the marsh near my house when he tried to run away after stealing a Monroe family heirloom."

"This story is so sad." Elena took the article from Sparrow. "And you said you've been seeing him out there lately."

"Yes, wandering in circles as if he's looking for something." Every time Sparrow remembered the way the Boy looked in the marsh, her stomach coiled.

"And you think he's looking for the heirloom?"

"Yep."

"So all you have to do is find it and return it to him," Elena said encouragingly.

"I already have. It's my watch."

"Your watch is the Monroes' family heirloom?" Elena's forehead furrowed. "That doesn't make sense."

Sparrow handed Elena the page from Mr. Monroe's book, *Orphan Trains: Small Towns, Big Hearts*.

Elena looked at the shredded edges. "Did you rip this out of a book?"

"Yes, but it doesn't matter. We have five more copies at home. Mr. Monroe gave me a copy and my aunt bought five at the charity auction. She loves the Monroes."

Elena's eyebrows shot up. "The ones who own the archives?"

"Yep. Long story." Sparrow pointed to the picture of the boy standing in the middle of the front row next to the other children. The pocket watch dangled from his hand. "That's my watch."

"Can I look closer?"

Sparrow handed Elena the photograph.

She studied the picture thoughtfully. "Is that what your ghost looks like?"

"Exactly."

Elena took a deep breath, as if she was trying to gather her feelings. "He looks really sad."

"I know."

"Wait, if he has the watch in this picture and the Monroes said he ran away with it, how did you end up with it?"

"That confused me too until I read the second article." Sparrow told Elena the Boy's complete story. "After he took his watch back, he ran away from the Monroes and somehow managed to make his way out to my house. It's really far and there is a lot of untamed land between our places. My house must have looked like a safe haven after all that wild. He hid on my front porch, but when he heard the barking of the hounds, he ran into the marsh to make them lose his scent. I think he must have dropped the watch or maybe even hidden it before running away from the dogs. He might have survived if the full moon hadn't caused a king tide."

Sadness clouded Elena's features and her voice got soft. "No wonder his soul has been trapped here."

Sparrow nodded, and both girls became quiet, almost reverent, as the meaning of Elena's words enveloped them.

"Sorry to interrupt." The girls looked up to see Eli standing at the door of the van. He wore jeans and a linen dress

245

shirt with the sleeves rolled up. His tattoo peeked out from under his sleeve, but he stood too far away for Sparrow to read the words.

"That's okay," Sparrow said. "I was showing Elena what I got from the Beulah archives." Sparrow handed Eli the newspaper articles.

He looked at them. "You thought to ask for copies? Well done. You have the instincts of a historian." Eli clapped Sparrow on the shoulder proudly, the way a father might.

On a different day, Sparrow would have been delighted by Eli's fatherly admiration, but in that moment, his paternal gesture reminded Sparrow of what she would never have.

Eli quickly scanned the article. "Of course, this sugar-coats the truth."

"What do you mean?" Sparrow asked.

"It doesn't mention that this child would be indentured to the Monroes until he was twenty-one. Some of these kids were forced to work for their adopting families without pay until they were old enough to leave."

Anger sizzled in Sparrow's belly. "That's not fair."

"No, but that's the way these placements worked. The children were given a home, and in return the kids became the property of the families that took them in. Everything they owned became the property of the adopting family. The families had to agree to treat the orphans as one of their own, but they didn't always honor their agreement. A lot of times the families never even adopted them officially, so technically some of these kids stayed orphans their entire lives. While some of the kids had happy endings, some didn't. It was the luck of the draw, and the children had no choice in the decision. It looks like this child had one of the unhappy endings."

"Wesley Monroe said the orphan they adopted stole from them and died in the marsh while trying to run away." The injustice of the entire situation shook Sparrow's core. It went against everything she knew to be right. The Boy's early death was tragic enough without his memory being tainted by a false accusation.

"If he risked the dangers of the marsh rather than staying with his adopting family, something must have made him desperate enough to leave."

Sparrow felt tears prick her eyes at the thought of the Boy suffering and quickly blinked them away before Eli noticed. Elena hadn't missed her reaction, though. She slipped her hand into Sparrow's and squeezed.

"He was wrongly accused," Sparrow said, wanting to set the record straight.

"These kids, especially the boys, were often treated with suspicion. They came from poor families in big cities. Occasionally, the country folks that took in these children thought their very natures were corrupt. Sometimes you still see that kind of prejudice toward inner-city kids, even today when people know better." Eli paused.

A sad quiet settled over the van. Sparrow felt like the marsh was listening to them tell the Boy's story.

"Do you think Mr. Monroe's ancestors lied about what happened? Mr. Monroe didn't even know what the family heirloom was. He said that part of the story had gotten lost over time."

"What is your theory?" Eli asked.

"I think the orphan ran away with his own heirloom, but the Monroes wanted it. So they claimed it belonged to them and that the orphan stole it."

"Could be. If there were any sort of wrongdoing on the Monroes' part, they wouldn't want to ruin the family's reputation by admitting it. People sometimes think it's easier to cover up injustice rather than apologize for it or make amends."

Sparrow nodded. That made sense. The Monroes were well respected and they were proud of their family name. Wrongly accusing a young boy in their care of stealing and then causing his death would be a blight on their reputation. She thought about the swirling spirits and the way they protected the grave. She had felt overwhelming sadness when she placed her hand on the tombstone, and now she knew why. The Boy had a heartbreaking story, and the spirits were acknowledging the sorrow of his death.

Sparrow could set things right. "I came for my watch."

"I thought you'd never ask." Eli handed Sparrow a velvet jewelry box.

"Is my watch in here?" The box was so fancy.

"It is. And I have some exciting news. It's a Patek Philippe."

"What is a Patek Philippe?"

"A watchmaker famous for the quality of its watches, and this one is a prime example. It is eighteen-carat gold, not brass or plate. Not only that, it has a solid gold wheel."

"What does that mean?"

"It means you should lock it up in a safety deposit box until you need a lot of money. That watch is worth a small fortune."

Sparrow opened the box. The watch had been polished to a high sheen, and it no longer looked like junk. "Small fortune? How much?"

"Depends on finding the right buyer, but . . ." Eli shrugged. "Enough to buy a big house, maybe more."

"Enough to buy a house?" Sparrow repeated dazedly.

Eli had just handed Sparrow a small fortune. Exactly what she needed to save Dalton House and the marsh.

CHAPTER TWENTY-NINE

Twilight had settled over Beulah by the time Sparrow got home.

Frogs croaked, fireflies flashed, and the moon shone over the marsh. Full and round, it dominated the sky like the sun's jealous sibling. She gazed up at the moon and thought about king tides and her Boy. Her heart lurched.

She knew what it felt like to have a voracious need to hold tight to the time before the sadness came. Sparrow wanted any shred of Mama she could get.

As she walked up the driveway, Sparrow tried to figure out how her plans had fallen apart. The day had started perfectly. She had found a daddy to love her, a plan to save Dalton House, friends, a way to help the Boy find peace, and the key to getting Mama back.

Everything she desired had been within her grasp, but it had unfurled like a spool of thread.

Sparrow clutched the pocket watch. She could either use it to save Dalton House and the marsh from destruction or give it to the Boy, and with that gesture, ensure Mama's return.

She slipped the watch into her pocket.

There was no choice. She wanted Mama back.

Sparrow walked into the kitchen to find Auntie Geraldine hanging up the phone.

Auntie Geraldine took one look at Sparrow, and her lips pulled into a thin, tight line.

Auntie Geraldine knew.

"How *could* you? You made a fool of yourself and me."

The embarrassment of the day swept over her like a flood. "I wouldn't have made that mistake if Mama hadn't left me with someone who hated me."

"You think I hate you?"

"I know it. You took everything I loved and ripped it to shreds like you said you would."

"How dare you accuse me of such a thing?"

Auntie Geraldine's denial made Sparrow furious. "You told the Castos they couldn't be friends with me."

"I wanted you to fit in with nice folks!"

"Like the Monroes?"

"*Yes*, exactly like them."

"You're selling Dalton House."

"You'll adjust."

"I won't."

"You'll have to. There's no other choice."

Sparrow pressed on. She wanted Auntie Geraldine to hear the full extent of her crimes.

"You threw away Mama's belongings."

"I donated them to charity. It's what's done when someone dies. Every time I walked by her room I saw reminders of her. She's *gone*. It's time to let her go."

"I can't." The ache in Sparrow's soul ran so deep she could barely breathe. She would never let Mama go. Never. She started to sob.

"Sparrow." Auntie Geraldine stepped toward her.

"Stay away from me." Sparrow stepped back.

Auntie Geraldine took another step toward Sparrow. "There are too many memories here. Too many distractions. You'll feel better once we leave this house."

Sparrow stepped back again. "I won't feel better until Mama comes back."

"*What?*" The color drained from Auntie Geraldine's face. She looked ashen. "You shouldn't want that."

"Why not? Other spirits do it. They come back."

"Are you referring to that ridiculous boy?"

Sparrow's whole body stiffened. "What do you know about him?"

"More than you think. You shouldn't wish his fate on your mama."

Sparrow glared at her aunt, thinking of all the times the Boy had teased her and Auntie Geraldine's reactions to him. Always, she was unperturbed and unafraid, as if she knew she had nothing to fear. Slowly, like the rise of the sun, realization dawned on Sparrow. She spat the words at Auntie Geraldine like an accusation. "You *see him*."

Auntie Geraldine shrugged.

"How long?" Sparrow demanded.

"Always."

"*Always?*" All this time, Auntie Geraldine could have helped her, talked to her about the Boy, talked to her about Mama. She could have been her friend, a confidant. Instead, she pretended she didn't see him. It was the worst of all of Auntie Geraldine's betrayals.

"And knowing about him, you still decided to sell the house and the land to Wesley Monroe for a *strip mall*?"

"It's for the best. You'll never be free of that ghost as long as you live here. Salt only does so much."

"*Salt?*" Sparrow asked incredulously.

Auntie Geraldine gave Sparrow a frosty look. "Yes, *salt*. It keeps spirits away. Why did you think it lined every window-sill and door? Did you think I had simply lost my mind?"

Sparrow had thought that. Now, she knew the truth. Auntie Geraldine was purposely trying to keep the Boy from her, and it was the final straw. Sparrow wouldn't let

Auntie Geraldine get away with it. She spied an envelope on the kitchen counter behind Auntie Geraldine. It looked like Mason Casto's papers. The ones that said he owned the 76 station. But these would say something different. They might be ownership papers for Dalton House. Sparrow lunged for them.

Auntie Geraldine sprang after Sparrow, but Sparrow was too quick.

"Those are important documents!"

Sparrow clutched the envelope. "Do these give Dalton House to the Monroes?"

Auntie Geraldine's face flushed red, and Sparrow knew they did.

Sparrow dashed into the yard with the envelope.

"Sparrow, bring those back here this instant!"

Sparrow let the screen door slam shut. She opened the envelope and pulled out the papers, ready to rip them to shreds.

Auntie Geraldine followed her. Her heels made loud clicking sounds on the hardwood. "Don't."

"Why shouldn't I?"

"Because Wesley will draw up more, and I'll sign them again." Auntie Geraldine walked toward Sparrow, hand outstretched.

Sparrow backed away. "It's my house. The Boy's house. Mama's house." Sparrow's voice cracked.

Auntie Geraldine moved closer. "It's not. It belonged to your mama and me. Now I'm the sole owner and I don't want to live here with that ghost and memories of your mama haunting my every step."

"But I do. Shouldn't that matter?" Sparrow looked toward her beloved marsh. If Auntie Geraldine sold it to the Monroes, it would all be gone. All of it. Tears rolled down her cheeks.

"You're a child. You don't know what's best." Auntie Geraldine pulled herself up to her full height and stalked toward Sparrow, hand outstretched. "Give me the papers."

Sparrow's vision blurred from her tears. She blinked them away and stared at the marsh. Her marsh. Dalton land. She belonged to it and it to her. Sparrow shut her eyes and pleaded with the marsh for help.

Like a benevolent father, it indulged her.

CHAPTER THIRTY

The marsh returned the Boy.

From her vantage point in the yard, Sparrow saw the marsh in its entirety. A bright, low-slung moon illuminated it with the vividness of midday. She saw the sandbar stretching from west to east, the mangrove trees on the far bank, and, deep within its depths, the Boy.

His presence lured Sparrow like a moth to a flame. This was her chance to turn the tide, to set everything right.

She just had to get past Auntie Geraldine. Auntie Geraldine stood before Sparrow, hand outstretched, demanding the papers.

Sparrow kicked Auntie Geraldine in the shin.

Auntie Geraldine doubled over, clutching her injured leg.

Sparrow pushed past her and sprinted toward the marsh. As she ran, she loosened her grip on the papers and the pages scattered before her like a flock of egrets.

"Sparrow!" Auntie Geraldine called, but Sparrow was beyond listening.

Sparrow splashed into the waters and ran until the sucking mud slowed her. She found the sandbar and began to make her way to the Boy. He shimmered in the moonlight like a beacon.

It was never quiet on the marsh at night. The loud croaking of the frogs overtook the crickets' softer song. Underneath the frogs' persistent yowls, the skittering movement of birds and other small animals reminded Sparrow of what she knew only too well. She wasn't the only living creature moving through the wetlands. Sparrow put thoughts of gators, snakes, and panthers from her mind and walked deeper into the marsh.

It was harder than she expected to navigate the marsh in the moonlight. The land she knew so well undulated with eerie shadows, and rain clouds crept toward the moon, threatening its light.

As she trudged forward, the shore got farther and farther away.

She continued to put distance between her and the land until she reached the Boy.

He wavered in the moonlight like a star.

She offered the watch to him. "Now you can help Mama."

The Boy smiled at Sparrow, but he made no move to take the watch from her.

She pushed it toward him. "Take it." He only needed to reach for it to seal their deal.

He looked toward the watch longingly, and then back at Sparrow. But he didn't make a move toward it.

She dangled it by the chain, allowing the gold to glint in the moonlight. "Don't you want it?"

He tipped his head to the side as if considering the question, but he did not reach for his family heirloom. He merely wavered in the moonlight, reminding Sparrow of the swirling spirits.

The snaking cold of doubt crept up Sparrow's spine and forced her to consider questions she preferred to leave unexplored. For the first time, Sparrow wondered if it wasn't the spirits who needed to learn how to be like the Boy, but the Boy who needed to learn how to be like them. What if *he* desired to exist in a different way? Did *he* long to let go of his ghostly form, so he could exist as a spirit untethered to the living world? Untethered to her.

Suddenly, everything Sparrow thought she knew shifted. Like gears finally clicking into place, she truly understood what the Boy needed. He needed to be released. He needed to leave the land of the living for the realm of spirits.

"Mama's not coming back, is she?"

The Boy gave no reply. He didn't need to. Sparrow already knew the answer.

She sank to the ground, exhausted and spent. She clutched the watch to her chest. She couldn't do it now. She couldn't give him the watch if Mama wasn't coming back. She couldn't lose everything—Mama, the Boy, Dalton House—and he wasn't asking her to. He was letting her choose his fate.

With no hope of Mama's return, the full weight of her sorrow pressed on her heart. Like a dam bursting, it gushed forth.

The Boy sat beside her as she poured her grief into the marsh. Her tears fell for the Boy, his loyalty and the sacrifice he was making for her, the father she didn't have, and Mama, who she would never see again in this lifetime.

He stayed by her side as she filled the marsh with her tears.

The marsh drank Sparrow's sorrow while a gentle breeze caressed her, and the whispering wind told her *love never says goodbye*, over and over again, until she began to believe it.

When she had spent her grief, the Boy beckoned to her, letting her know it was time to return to where she belonged.

Thunder cracked, and a black storm cloud rolled over the massive moon, plunging the marsh into darkness. Her time of sanctuary had ended. The marsh was changing from benevolent father to wild thing again, reminding her she was a girl, not a nighttime creature of the marsh.

Thunder cracked again, and it started to pour.

The Boy urged her to hurry. Suddenly, he was panicked, and Sparrow realized why. The tide was rising—*rapidly*.

Sparrow recalled the gigantic, low-slung moon and the warnings she'd grown up hearing. Her skin prickled as she thought *king tide*.

Fear twisted Sparrow's stomach.

She took in her surroundings, trying to determine her distance from shore. She saw the big oak tree that marked the edge of the marsh, a dark shadow barely visible against the black night sky. She was deep in the marsh with a surging king tide, and her only path to shore was a sand bridge that would soon cease to exist.

The Boy's fate was about to become hers.

Sparrow slipped the watch into her pocket and ran.

The Boy appeared in front of her, disappearing and reappearing every few feet, a spectral guide leading her home. He was doing for Sparrow what he had been unable to do for himself. He was saving her.

Sparrow felt the water rise.

At first, the water only splashed over her feet and she ran along like a child in the surf. Then it crested her ankles and rose to midcalf, the weight of the water dragging her down, making it difficult to move.

The Boy stayed always ahead, lighting her way, but the sandbar stretching from Beulah to the sea was descending into the depths of the marsh like a sinking ship.

CHAPTER THIRTY-ONE

Sparrow ran as fast as she could.

Though the oak trees on the bank were becoming larger, letting her know she was closer to shore, she still had far to go, and the tide's response to the moon was quicker than her feet.

Even with the Boy's help, she veered too far off the sandbar—a fatal mistake. Instead of silty sand to give her feet purchase, she ran through slippery reed grass that twisted and coiled around her legs, slowing her.

As she reached down to untangle her feet, she heard her name being called.

"Sparrow!"

She never thought she'd be happy to hear her name being yelled by Auntie Geraldine. Her heart fluttered with hope at the sound of her aunt's stern, determined call. "Auntie Geraldine! I'm here!"

Sparrow reached down with both hands to disentangle

her feet, frantic to get away, but the slick knot of reed grass only tightened. "Auntie Geraldine!"

Again came the answering call, "Sparrow!"

A flood of light shone her way as a flashlight beam swung frantically in her direction.

Before Sparrow could answer again, her hand released a clump of grass, but instead of setting her free, she lost her balance and pitched forward into the water.

Water flowed over her head and into her mouth. Sparrow tried to kick free, but the more she did, the more trapped she became.

She fought upward, caught a breath of life-sustaining air, and then went under again. She opened her eyes against the brackish water. The Boy floated at her feet, trying to untangle them, but his ghostly efforts were no match for the living marsh. The Boy could flash lights and move things around, but his powers were limited and unable to unravel complicated knots.

Sparrow reached for her feet and began to work.

The Boy disappeared.

Sparrow pushed up for another breath of air, but couldn't reach the surface. As she sank again, the Boy reappeared above her, a lighthouse beacon to give her hope.

Sparrow's lungs were on fire, but she needed air, not

water, to extinguish the pain, and she fought with her body to not take the breath it so desperately wanted.

Just when she thought she'd lost the fight, the marsh gave Sparrow one last gift—Auntie Geraldine.

Auntie Geraldine's strong hands found Sparrow and pulled her up.

For once, Sparrow understood the benefit of Auntie Geraldine's height. Her long legs gave her an advantage in the rising water. What measured as chest high for Sparrow barely hit Auntie Geraldine's waist.

Auntie Geraldine gave a mighty yank and Sparrow came free of the reed grass.

Auntie Geraldine scooped Sparrow out of the water and carried her to shore.

When they got to the bank, Auntie Geraldine set Sparrow down gently under one of the great oaks, and then collapsed next to her.

The Boy stood at the border between water and land, shimmering dimly in the pouring rain.

"I thought you were going to drown," Auntie Geraldine said in short, ragged gulps.

"You saved me." Wonder and relief overtook Sparrow. Auntie Geraldine had risked her life to rescue Sparrow.

"I was only able to because of him." Auntie Geraldine pointed at the Boy. "He shone above you like a lighthouse."

Sparrow watched the Boy flicker. She owed him her life and much more. "Why didn't you tell me you could see him?"

"*Why would I?* I spent my entire childhood ignoring that ghost, hoping that if I did he'd go away. And you know what? Eventually, he did. Then you came along and that boy was back. Letting you know I could see him would only encourage you and him. The two of you were bad enough already. That ghost followed you around like a dog and *you liked him* . . ." Auntie Geraldine sucked in a breath. She seemed to be deciding what to say next. How much more to say. "All my life, all I've ever wanted to be was a regular person. Seeing that ghost . . . I wanted to be like everyone else, not some flea market psychic."

For the first time, Sparrow glimpsed the Auntie Geraldine Mama knew. The lonely one. "I like flea market psychics."

"You would." Even though Auntie Geraldine's words were curt, Sparrow heard something in her voice she'd never noticed before—warmth.

The rain began to slow and Sparrow watched the Boy waver, his hair and clothing unaffected by the weather.

"Why do we see him?"

"I don't know."

"Do you see other spirits?" Sparrow wondered how alike she and Auntie Geraldine were.

The rain slowed to a trickle and the moon started to peek out from behind the clouds.

"Those swirly wisps? I try not to."

"I think Mama is one of the wispy spirits now."

"Maybe," Auntie Geraldine said thoughtfully.

"I wasn't ready for her to leave me." Sparrow choked on the words.

"She wasn't ready to leave you either. She fought hard to stay with you as long as she could, but it was her time. We don't get to make that choice for ourselves." Auntie Geraldine's breath caught. "She thought she left you in good hands."

Sparrow's throat ached and tears slid down her cheeks. It warmed her heart and hurt it to the point of breaking that Mama tried so hard to stay with her.

"I don't hate you," Auntie Geraldine said.

"I don't hate you either, but I wish you were nicer to me."

Auntie Geraldine swallowed and her voice got tight. "I meant to be, but being around you was harder than I expected. Lord have mercy, I loved your mama, and you remind me so much of her. It's like living with a different kind of ghost."

Sparrow *wished* the mirror reminded her she was Lilly Dalton's daughter. "But I look nothing like Mama."

"No, but you are like her in every other way . . . brave,

strong, loving. Your heart is as big and wide as that marsh out there. Just like your mama's. You see the world in ways others don't. When you look at that boy, you don't see a ghost. You see a friend. Same as with the Castos. And Dalton House; I wish I saw what you see when you look at it. You're like your mama. Seeing beauty where others don't. You inherited all the best parts of her. I see her in you every day . . ." Auntie Geraldine fell silent. She was crying.

Sparrow's eyes stung and her heart swelled to the point of bursting to hear Auntie Geraldine talk about her in that way. Like she loved her. Hearing how much she was like Mama made Sparrow's whole body throb with hurt, but in a way that felt like being put back together instead of being torn apart.

Sparrow reached for Auntie Geraldine's hand. She missed Mama too, and Sparrow wanted to put her back together a little bit, if she could. "You remind me of her sometimes. When you smile, you look like Mama."

Auntie Geraldine took a big breath. "One of the last things your mama said to me was, you're going to need that girl and she's going to need you. Don't be stubborn about it." Auntie Geraldine's voice got crackly and she put Sparrow's hand in her lap. "She was always right about matters of the heart."

The rain stopped and the clouds slid off the moon. From somewhere up high, a whip-poor-will started calling. Soon, all the animals would shake off the rain and come out of hiding.

"I wonder if we can start over? I'll probably always be snippy, but I do have it in me to love you the way your mama wanted me to. I promise I'll love you like that from now on."

That sounded pretty good to Sparrow. She laid her head on Auntie Geraldine's shoulder.

"I'll take that for a yes."

Sparrow nodded. Her cheek rubbed against Auntie Geraldine's dress. The feel of cotton against her skin reminded Sparrow of laying her head against Mama when the preacher got long-winded and the nave felt like a steaming shower.

"Will you work on the snippy part?"

"If I have to." Sparrow heard something else in Auntie Geraldine's voice she'd never noticed before—humor. Auntie Geraldine had made a joke.

They stayed like that for a moment, listening to the marsh coming out of hiding and settling into their new way of being together.

Auntie Geraldine cleared her throat and helped Sparrow to her feet. "We should go up to the house and get dry clothes."

Sparrow felt the weight of the watch in her pocket. She looked at the Boy wavering in the moonlight. "Just a second."

Sparrow walked to the edge of the marsh where the Boy stood. She pulled out the pocket watch. She clicked it open and wound the crown. She held it to her ear and heard the steady ticking. She marveled at the miracle of it. She didn't know how or why it still worked. But it did. With it, she could save Dalton House and keep the Boy by her side.

She looked at her friend. The Boy looked like he always did. Black pants too short, boots unlaced with the tongues flapping. He had died in the marsh, trying to hold on to a piece of his old life. And more than anyone, Sparrow understood why, but she also knew the sadness it had brought him. He'd gotten stuck in place. He couldn't go back and he couldn't go forward. If Sparrow kept his watch to save Dalton House, she'd be trapping him in his sorrow forever. He'd never be allowed to move on. Never find peace.

Sparrow drew back her arm and hurled the watch deep into the depths of the marsh.

She heard the sound of the watch hitting the water and reached for the Boy's hand. It felt like trying to hold mist.

Wispy spirits began to gather around him. They alighted on him, landing on his arms and shoulders like dewdrops.

More and more wispy spirits encircled the Boy, and Sparrow knew they were coming to guide him home.

Sparrow released his hand.

With a touch that felt like the fluttering of butterfly wings, the Boy kissed Sparrow's cheek.

And he was gone.

CHAPTER THIRTY-TWO

The morning after the Boy left, Sparrow found the papers from Wesley Monroe strewn all over the yard. She picked them up and gave them to Auntie Geraldine. Auntie Geraldine said she had finally started to see Dalton House the way Sparrow and Mama did and threw the papers in the trash. They were staying at Dalton House.

That same day, Maeve and Johnny came to see Sparrow, and together they walked down to the marsh. Sparrow told them everything that happened after she left the party. Johnny listened in his quiet way, while Maeve voiced disappointment that she'd missed it all.

Sparrow told Maeve she was sorry she wasn't a Casto, and Maeve told Sparrow to stop being ridiculous. She said she had too many cousins already. She said it was better to be friends with a Dalton than to be related to one, and just like that, the divide between them vanished.

About a week after the Boy left, Sparrow asked Maeve and Johnny to meet her at the graveyard.

Sparrow arrived early with flowers for Mama's grave. Auntie Geraldine had offered to get Sparrow cut roses, but she declined. Sparrow knew Mama would prefer the messy perfection of the flowers she gathered along her way.

Sparrow placed the flowers at Mama's headstone and scrunched them together until they looked right. She still ached for Mama. A part of Sparrow would always miss her. But Sparrow knew she would eventually see Mama again, when it was Sparrow's turn to become a wispy spirit. Until then, Sparrow was going to live the way Mama would want her to—striving to see beauty where others did not.

When Johnny and Maeve arrived, Sparrow led them to the swamp-touched gravestone.

Waiting beside it were Auntie Geraldine, Miss Ruby, Eli, Elena, and the Monroes.

Maeve waved enthusiastically at Elena and Eli. "I thought they left town."

"I asked them to stay on for a few days, and they agreed," Sparrow said.

Then Maeve noticed the Monroes. She squeezed Sparrow's arm. "What are *they* doing here?"

"I invited them," Sparrow said simply.

"Why?" Maeve asked.

"It's Sparrow's gathering, Maeve. She can invite whoever she wants," Johnny said.

Maeve huffed.

"They have a good reason for being here. You'll see." Sparrow led Maeve and Johnny to the gravestone.

When they got there, Sparrow pointed at the headstone. The Boy's name had been etched on it, and underneath his name, the words *Beloved Son, Loyal Friend, Brave Soul* had been inscribed in the granite. At the base of the tombstone there was a statue of a lamb.

"That's real nice," Johnny said.

"It really is." Maeve reached out and ran her hand over the Boy's grave, but no swirling spirits encircled her this time. Now that the Boy was at peace, the spirits seemed to be at peace too.

"Eli figured out the Boy's name. Auntie Geraldine arranged the inscription, and the Monroes added the lamb." Sparrow had told Mr. Monroe the Boy's story and she was surprised to find an ally in him. He agreed it was time for his family to make amends. Sparrow suggested a service for the Boy, and Mr. Monroe offered to purchase a lamb for his grave.

Auntie Geraldine and Sparrow had already decided they should be the ones in charge of the inscription because they knew him best.

When Sparrow mentioned to Miss Ruby that she was planning a service for the Boy, filling her in on the story of his life, not on the ghostly part of his existence, Miss Ruby offered to preside over it. As it turned out, Miss Ruby was an associate pastor at her church. She didn't preach every Sunday, but filled in on occasion.

Miss Ruby did a wonderful job. The Boy had a lovely service filled with comforting words and old country hymns.

Afterward, Sparrow walked Elena and Eli to their van.

Elena slipped a piece of paper into Sparrow's hand and gave her fingers an affectionate squeeze. "I couldn't leave without giving you my address. I foresee a visit to New York in your future."

"Thank you." Sparrow loved the idea of visiting Elena in New York.

"We'd love to have you and your aunt come visit us sometime," Eli said. He had taken off the sport coat he wore during the Boy's service and rolled up his sleeves. Sparrow was close enough that she could finally read the tattoo on his arm. The words *Love never says goodbye* were written in sloping script.

Sparrow's heart skipped a beat. She pulled the picture of Mama out of her back pocket. She may have accepted her death, but she still hung on to her memories. She turned the picture over and looked at the words on the back, even though she knew them by heart.

"What do you have there?" Eli asked.

A marsh breeze blew, wrapping Sparrow in the scent of Beulah. She smiled and slid the photograph into her back pocket. "A history puzzle for the future."

Eli nodded. "Those are my favorite kind."

Sparrow hugged Elena goodbye.

As the periwinkle van began to drive away, Sparrow joined Auntie Geraldine. Auntie Geraldine put her arm around Sparrow's shoulder and pulled her close. "I suppose you'll want to visit New York."

"I will. But when I do, we'll go together."

The setting sun illuminated Auntie Geraldine, casting her in a warm glow. Auntie Geraldine wasn't Mama, but Sparrow knew she was the next best thing. Beside Auntie Geraldine were Maeve, Johnny, Miss Ruby, and the Monroes—Sparrow's Beulah family

ACKNOWLEDGMENTS

I owe a deep debt of gratitude to my amazing agent, generous mentor, and cherished friend, Laura Rennert, and the whole Andrea Brown family, especially: Andrea Brown, Caryn Wiseman, Lara Perkins, and Jennifer March Soloway. To a woman, they are fierce, smart, and loyal, and I feel incredibly lucky to be included in their circle of love.

I truly believe fate brought my brilliant, lovely editor, Mallory Kass, into my life. I see her guiding hand on every page. She made this book better, and I am so thankful she loves tarot cards and believes in ghosts—or does not *not* believe in ghosts. Mostly, I'm thankful that she believed in this story enough to give it a home at Scholastic. For that, I will always, always be grateful.

Without my sister, Beth, there would be just page after page of words, words, words, and no book. She is my first and last reader, my champion, my cheerleader, my confidant, and my best friend. Thanks seems too meager of a word for all the late-night edit sessions, advice, childcare, encouragement, laughter, tough love, and love-love, but I know she knows how deep my gratitude runs, because that's the thing about sisters, they just know.

I am fortunate to have an interesting, quirky, funny family that likes to talk. Their stories—often wonderfully exaggerated—inspire me in big and small ways. Over the years, my family has expanded and our hodgepodge of connections and intersections make the love feel bigger. I am especially thankful for the support of my mom, Elizabeth; my dad, Joel; my sister, Angie; my cousin, Storm; my brother-in-law, Per; my mother-in-law, Kate; and my grandfather, Tom, and my grandmother, Clarice, who are no longer with us, but whose love has never said goodbye.

Most of all, I am grateful to my husband, David Piontek, who can fix anything, even a bad day; my son, William, whose insightful poet's soul makes being in his presence restful; my daughter, Clarice, whose unending optimism lifts my spirit in even the darkest moments; and little Gavin, who is no longer so little, but whose carefree happiness always makes me smile.

ABOUT THE AUTHOR

Victoria Piontek spent her childhood on the east coast of Florida listening to her mother's stories of strong southern women, family secrets, and ghosts. She now lives in Northern California. *The Spirit of Cattail County* is her first novel.